As Lie Is to Grin

As Lie Is to Grin

Simeon Marsalis

Catapult   New York

This is a work of fiction. All of the characters, organizations, and events portrayed in this novel are either products of the author's imagination or used fictitiously.

Photographs on pages 12, 28, and 39 by Thomas Visser. Photographs on pages 142 and 146 from Special Collections, University of Vermont Libraries.

Published by Catapult
catapult.co

ISBN: 978-1-936787-59-3

Catapult titles are distributed to the trade by Publishers Group West
Phone: 866-400-5351

Library of Congress Control Number: 2016952068

Printed in the United States of America

9 8 7 6 5 4 3 2 1

RED HERRING:

1. A smoked herring, which is turned red by the smoke.

2. *Something unimportant that is used to stop people from noticing or thinking about something important.*

As Lie Is to Grin

Prologue

The path wound upward and to the left, so I climbed. The institution then appeared from behind a row of trees. As I passed the driveway, two security guards sitting in a white booth were visible in the near distance. My heartbeat quickened. "I should not be here." My fingers fidgeted with the sheet of paper in my pocket, which was creased from being folded over and over. I felt ashamed. I began to slip from the present to the day we met, and at that moment there was a call from the sky. I searched the space beneath the falling sun. My eyes gleaned a solitary crow. It had separated from its murder. As I smiled and lowered my head, you were emerging from the school's main entrance. Melody. I took the letter from my pocket and walked forward.

I was up late into the evening, researching the University of Vermont, where I was enrolled for the fall semester. I feared that my college decision had been made under false pretenses. This belief was causing me a great deal of discomfort, so I had gone on the school's website to convince myself it was not true, when I stumbled on a page entitled "Student Dissent." It began with an introduction—"1969, to the delight of many students and chagrin of many alumnae, Kake Walk was interred"—that reminded me of a novel I had tried to compose (and was now attempting to forget). I opened my notebook to the prologue and six subsequent chapters. They were all incomplete. Each semiautobiographical sketch muddled the line between my life and my fiction. I could not find meaning in the one or the other—did not divine a reason to resolve my real issues by way of text. I closed the notebook and looked back to the phone, as I had interpreted this connection as a sign to continue reading. The bulk of the article consisted of three alumni biographies. Crystal joined a sorority in 1947 and was made a dissenting student when the national organization decided to disband the chapter for granting a black woman the right to pledge. Bonnie attended from 1969 to 1973 and helped to oust the Army's ROTC program from campus. Carmen graduated in 1992 and feared that the push for multiculturalism she initiated with her fellow students had not amounted to any change at all. As the record became increasingly futile, I was distracted by a sound from the road. The lights of a car flashed into my window.

Everything went temporarily white. I pulled the blinds closed. The front gate opened. Footsteps descended the staircase. There was a knock at my bedroom door, but I did not answer. My sleep patterns were interrupted by cloudy dreams. I left in the morning, without rousing my mother.

Act
I

There was a copy of the school newspaper at the end of a long table in the student center, dated August 31, 2010. I flipped the paper open and spilled some coffee on the page 1 article. It gave information about my class—fourteen countries, forty states, 10 percent ALANA (Asian American, Latino, African American, Native American, and Multiracial)—and made me feel part of some experiment that was in its beginning stages. I passed the article about the ROTC fitness test result and realized that Bonnie's efforts to ban the Army program had been temporarily effective. On the next page there was an article entitled "SGA President Pushes for Transparent Registration: Book Prices and Syllabuses to Be Made Available Earlier."

The president was looking above his head to the left, typing at a computer screen. His mouth was slightly open and his skin stood out against the white walls around him. Just inside a room on the other side of the building I was now sitting in, our Student Government Association's president had had his picture taken. I could not avoid feeling there was something important about this article that I was missing. I left the cafeteria in a haze and continued down College Street to South Willard Street, which became North, and stopped at number 42; two brown-haired men were smoking a joint on the porch.

"Is Mark here?"

"He's in the living room."

Three couches lined the walls. There were glasses and coffee mugs full of brown liquids on all of the surfaces, along with muddy clothes strewn on the floor. Two stripes, one red and one blue, were painted around the bedroom doorways, wrapped into the kitchen, and ended in a purple blob. I heard footsteps coming down the stairs.

"David!"

"What's up?" As he went to hug me, our cheeks touched, and I felt his smile, unnecessarily wide, against my face. He had been my group leader for orientation in the spring, and we bonded over smoking weed, which Mark assumed I did. He pulled a bong out from behind the couch, calling the two men from the porch, and introduced me to Matt and Luke from Massachusetts and Maryland.

"Jimmy signed the lease. We call it the Rib Shack."

"The house?"

"Yeah, it's called Jimmy's Rib Shack. You have to meet him, dude. He's fucking crazy. We don't know if Tom-Tom is coming back."

"Who?"

"Didn't I tell you about him?" Mark rose as he was speaking and sped through the hallway to the kitchen, returning with four twelve-ounce cans of 4 percent beer decorated with an American flag. "You may be able to crash in his bedroom. There are two upstairs, two more in here, one attached to the kitchen, five in total." But Jimmy had not returned after two hours, so I finished my beer and excused myself from the Rib Shack, after taking two shots of whiskey from a plastic 1.75-liter container.

Walking down Pearl Street, past the liquor outlet and tattoo parlor, perspiration gathered on my chest. It had hovered around 80 degrees all day. I passed a salon where women stood braiding hair, heading toward the walking path that wound around Lake Champlain for miles. I looked down at my phone and typed,

"Population, Burlington Vermont, jobs," and found some business "quick facts" from the 2007 census. "Women-owned firms 25%, Black-owned firms 1.3%, American Indian and Native Alaskan–owned firms S"—which, I decided, meant too small a number to count. I turned left, looking south at the glass façade of the ecological center with its two rectangular wings. One of them had a design resembling a giant eyeball from the distance. As my gaze shifted right, I saw that the sky was turning vibrant pink behind the Adirondacks. The town was flanked by two mountain ranges. As I left the walking path and went back up the hill toward the Green Mountains of Vermont, the campus seemed to be encircled by a translucent bubble. I was sure the image was an illusion brought on by the diminishing light and the cones in my eyes, but when I blinked the mirage did not go away.

I brushed my teeth in the bathroom across from the staircase in the middle of the second floor of Patterson Hall. There were three other young men there, so I handled my affairs quickly, returning to stare at my sleeping roommate, Gary. I dressed and made my way to French.

Once outside of my dorm, I stared at the collection of buildings called Redstone Campus. They seemed to have been built without regard for previous style. I logged into www.uvm.edu /~campus/tour/archhistory.html and browsed a page that revealed the campus buildings' architectural firms, periods, and dates of erection. Passing Southwick Music Hall, I learned that a

firm from New York, McKim, Meade & White, had fashioned it in the Colonial Revival style (1934). Not the extension (1975), that was influenced by Brutalism. I had come across the name of the firm last year, and this seemed some sign to continue searching, but as I scrolled through all of the dates and styles hastily, I was struck with the guilt of living upon land that was stolen and constructed on in the style of other places so far away.

In class, I stared at the side of a young woman's face. Every time Madame Paulette called on Delilah she would jump as if unprepared. She sat in the first row by the first aisle. I kept looking, from the third row by the third aisle to the front of the classroom. There was a moment when she craned her neck back as if to stretch; I was so attentive that, as she moved, I did as well. Delilah recognized me, though we had not met before. I tried to catch her as the class was dismissed but didn't make it around a heavyset Vermonter named Tim, who told Paulette in French that he loved her Québécoise accent. As I left Waterman, Delilah was already walking down College Street.

I found myself in the crosswalk on Main Street. It was unnervingly empty. Clouds did not race by—they hung there, still, against a southern breeze. No cars approached, so I imagined three trucks pressing forward, wrenching my body from my neck.

There was a copy of *The Cynic* from last week, dated September 7, 2010, on a chair in the Dining Hall of the student center. I read the front page, "LGBTQ Awesome," staring at the three pictures: the bronze statue of a mountain lion draped in a rainbow flag, students sitting around a table with two rainbow flags draped over it, and another of the same students jumping, with a rainbow flag above their heads, directly in front of Lafayette Hall. An article on page 3, "Debate Sparks over SGA President's Summer Stipend," featured one of the students from the pictures. It read, "(President) receives a stipend of $175 per week during the summer and some SGA Senators do not believe he earned it. Though he was not convicted of wrong-doing, the Chair of the Public Relations Committee had this to say, 'I think collectively the majority of us can say we are disappointed with what you did this summer . . . I think our expectations were poorly conveyed. You did do something wrong because, in our eyes, you didn't do what we wanted.'" It was our SGA president. He was standing next to a podium, defending his actions against the dubious criticism of his white colleagues. As I stared at the photo, I began to feel attacked. This was an irrational reaction, I thought, based on the similarities between our skin tones, so I closed the newspaper and left the Davis Center (Postmodern), traversing the green behind the Physical Science building (International) toward the Annex (Postmodern), which was attached to the Old Mill (Federal), which had been reconstructed (High Victorian Gothic) with funds from John P. Howard, before crossing the green to Waterman (Colonial Revival), where I now thought the buildings that first appeared to mock one another were definitely part of some interminable chain that the website had not recorded.

I entered Delilah's name into the Internet browser on my phone. It returned "Sampson and Delilah," the biblical story about a woman colluding to cut a man's hair and drain him of his powers. The story stayed with me through French class, after which I made a joke about her name that she did not find funny. "Can I have your number?" I asked. "I might need some help with the French . . ."

"Sure, sure." She wrote the numbers, the same way Melody had, before walking down the hallway, looking back once, and exiting up the stairwell. I took a drink from the water fountain, which was tan and shaped like the number 8, then stared at the grate covering the drain. The fire bell went off, interrupting my daydream.

The sun was beginning to set, so I walked to Williams Hall before it did. Fifteen students sat on the fire escape, watching clouds turn purple, the sky above the horizon divided into orange and yellow stripes. It was a cool evening. The summer was becoming fall. In the Rib Shack, Mark took a framed poster of a man staring at a frame of himself—staring at a frame of himself, ad infinitum— off of the wall. That was the sign Adderall, cocaine, or ketamine were being snorted. A few upperclassmen visited the house, all still bronzed from the summer; some of them talked about jumping into waterfalls at the Bolton Potholes. I thought of the pressure of falling liquid, an undercurrent, which made me think of my mother, Doris, and her fear of water. I sat across from James, Luke, Mark, and Matthew and began to drink whiskey with them, not paying attention to any other activity in the house. Luke and Matthew tried to consume as much as Mark, but none could hold alcohol like James. As the night wore on, though, and James continued to drink, he regressed to infantile outbursts. Within a few hours, he had chewed the center out of a piece of bread and was sticking his penis through it. I had never seen a white man's penis. There was something artistic in the way he was thrusting into the bread, how the ridge of the head pushed against the little cinnamon raisins.

SEPTEMBER 17, 2010

I had decided to get something to eat before spending Friday afternoon in the library. I walked to the cafeteria between Harris and Millis that students had taken to calling the Grundle, which was slang for *perineum*. The cafeteria on Redstone Campus would be closed all fall, so students who purchased the same meal plan and lived in twenty-three residential halls crammed into this dining room for each meal. The line stretched out the door to the parking lot, and I was forced into conversation with the student in front of me, who was from Long Island as well. We spoke about bloated class sizes. I tried to excuse myself, but he followed me to a table and said that we should exchange numbers because our hometowns were so close together. I chose to leave when he excused himself to go to the bathroom, and walked across campus to the library.

On the second floor, I sat at a public computer and followed the link from the school's website to the site of a company that managed all of the university's virtual classrooms. In each tab, you could find select readings and videos from topics related to your class syllabus. I clicked on English 023 and scrolled down to September 20, 2010. The week's heading was "American Modernism: Stein, Hemingway, Fitzgerald." I read excerpts from *Melanctha*, *A Farewell to Arms*, and *This Side of Paradise.* In the Extra Readings tab, I could see that the teacher had suggested Jean Toomer's 1920s masterpiece *Cane*, placing it under the subheading "Harlem Renaissance." Instead of reading, I logged on to the registrar's page and withdrew from the class, before gathering my things for Delilah's.

I touched her back, gently.

"Why are you moving your fingers so slow?"

"Relax."

"Stop trying so hard."

We laid the mattress on the floor and threw a collection of blankets next to it so we could roll around on a homemade queen. I ran my fingers down her spine, this time even more slowly. With my other hand I reached for the smartphone Melody's father was still paying for and shut off the volume. There was nothing I liked about the songs left on the phone. Rick was into black music from the late 1970s and the mid-1980s: Michael Jackson hits, pop tunes whose soul was stamped out for digital reproduction. I put my left hand on Delilah's hip, and she stroked the ribs beneath my armpit. I listened to her breathing. She asked me to put on a condom, and I did, as she balanced her elbows on the pillows. Her heart rose toward me. Her right hand beckoned me forward. She grabbed my penis, placing it inside her, bringing that same right hand to the back of my neck. As she felt me become tense, she whispered into my ear, "Come," pulling at what was inside me. After she had gone to sleep, I stared at the back of her hair, which was cut and straightened into a bob. A dream catcher hung from a nail above the center of her light blue duvet. I fell asleep. In the middle of the night, something hit me on the back of the head. She asked, "Did you piss the bed?"

"I sweat sometimes when I sleep."

I asked her where the towels were.

"You should just shower at your house."

"I was going to put them on top of the sheets."

"It's all right. Please shower at your house." I looked at her again, and she began to smile. "I'm joking, the towels are in the closet." I smiled, too, and climbed on top of her, swelling; her moan was singing.

I was trying to make the maintenance of my teeth a ritual again. My mind began to wander back to the writer's workshop I took in high school, then to Melody, so I was repeating the phrase "pearly whites" to myself as toothpaste fell into the sink. While the hot water ran, I thought about my roommate and my concerns became more present. Gary and I had spoken on only one occasion. He inquired: "Where is my ramen?" "Are you good at basketball?" "Do you want to join my intramural team?" I answered "I don't know" to these few questions. He looked at me and then trudged down the hallway. This morning he was lying next to the radiator, and something about the calmness of his sleep upset me. I left the dorm room and circled the periphery of campus to get to class and bypassed the other students, whose expressions would remind me of Gary's.

Victorian fraternity houses dotted South Prospect Avenue. I stopped for a moment at number 282. The oak front doors stood around twelve feet tall with golden handles. American flags covered the windows on the first floor, and the sky behind the fraternity house was gray. I could see the outline of one horse-headed cloud, but none of the others was well defined. In the single window at the top of the house, the vision of a young man dressed in a gray three-piece suit appeared. He bent over what seemed to be a bed, made it, and then sat, before placing a pen in the side of his mouth. The sighting of this vaguely familiar man so upset me that I cast my eyes down all the way to the green between Waterman and Old Mill. The sudden feeling that this year was unfolding in the same way as last year overtook me. So I rose and walked east until I entered Jeffords Hall, where the empty glass atrium calmed me. I could see the Stafford Greenhouse from where I was standing, so I walked in that direction to see the flora that cost hundreds of thousands of dollars a year to manicure. It reminded me of the garage at my mother's house. As I tried to open the front door, a line from *Cane* came to me: "The dead house is stuffed. The stuffing is alive. It is sinful to draw one's head out of live stuffing in a dead house."

Chapter 1

There was a family of deer grazing in the neighbors' yard. The leaves had nearly vanished. Dried and rust-colored remnants still stuck to some branches. I watched the seasons change from our living room window. Doris rolled out of her room at 5:45 p.m. and put the water to boil, before grabbing a plastic bottle of marinara sauce from the fridge. I picked up the newspaper from the table. She didn't get it often, but since America was considering a black presidential candidate, she had been buying New York's Times, Post, *and* Daily News. *I flipped through articles— "Memorial Dedicated at African Burial Ground," "Feds Waited Weeks to Warn on Tainted Meat," "Sean Bell's Fiancée Cheers New Sobriety Test for Cops"—without any intention. Toward the end of the classifieds, I saw a funny little ad. The typeface was gothic and declared "Daily Planet Writer's Workshop." The listed phone number was 1-800-WRITING, and no credits were transferable to or from any nationally accredited high school or university.*

"May I take writing classes?"

"That depends on what it costs."

"May I use your computer?"

"Yes." Doris didn't move. I walked toward her room. "Where do you think you're going?"

"To your room."

"What did I tell you about going into my room?"

"But you're cooking."

"So wait. What is the hurry?"

I stopped in the hallway. "Can I just—"

"Sit down!" Then she spoke to herself. "These disrespectful fucking men. Not only do I have to cook, but I have to be a computer, and it all has to happen at once? You try to raise them right, treat them with respect, but no matter what, they always come back to you, ungrateful boys."

After finishing her dinner, Doris got her computer and placed it in front of me. I went to www.dailypworkshop.com. The program had four tiers—Beginning, Building, Mature, and Novelist. You had to take three months of classes in the first two tiers (poetry, fiction, creative nonfiction), and four months in the second two. Three months cost $349.99 in the first two, $449.99 for the second two. All of this I showed to my aunt on the screen. She said she would pay for nine months of classes, before reminding me that we were to have visitors this evening. I finished the pasta. I cleaned the living room as the sun was descending. She went into the garage and came back upstairs after an hour. The bell rang.

The night was thick. From the porch light, I could make out a middle-aged couple through the gate. Worry in the wife's soul hung over each slight movement, from the way she smiled, timidly, to the way she clenched and let go of her husband's hand. I invited them into the living room, where my mother sat staring through the back window. As we approached, her eyes remained transfixed on some point beyond the glass. She said, "You have not been truthful with each other," turning to face them.

"How did you know?"

To which my aunt replied, "We know these things," as she turned back to the window. Every slight movement was an act she performed until the end of each session, when Doris opened the garage to a patch of flowers—carnations, catchfly, lilies, and scarlet sage.

"How do they grow without light?" her patients would ask.

"That is the miracle," she would say. "I go out to the forest by the highway, and I find the strongest wildflowers. The plants live in the garage during the winter with insufficient light." In truth, she packed boxes of flowers in green cartons from the florist and arranged them before we were to receive her patients. Doris always referenced "this little patch of meadow, in this little patch of wood," where she supposedly spent most of her weekends, digging up flowers that could grow strong anywhere. She told me, "They usually don't believe it. That does not matter. The flowers give them hope in this country where there is none."

The front page of the school paper announced, "University Receives 146 Million . . . Our faculty's success in attracting a record amount of research funding is a strong measure of the University's significant advance over the last decade . . . Award amounts have grown 96% since 2000 when sponsored awards were $75 million." I passed advertisements for Stowe's ski resort to "Students Can't Mask Joy for Latino Heritage Month . . . Students who participated in the mask making said they came away with broadened horizons and paint-stained clothes." One remarked that mask making was a fun way to get into someone else's culture. I stopped on page 7, at "New UVM Magazine Gaining Popularity Among Dissatisfied Artists," looking at a picture of a brown-haired woman sitting on a porch with a pen in her mouth. It was the same pose I had seen the man in the gray suit strike. I suffered the distinct feeling that my mind was colluding with the paper to mock me. I folded the newspaper, put it in my bag, and gathered the rest of my things to go downtown.

It was Mark's friend Jimmy's sometimes girlfriend Emma's birthday party. We sat in the Vietnamese restaurant at a long table with two handles of whiskey and ginger ale. I sipped at my cup and tried not to watch my fellow students too closely. Eight people ordered the number 7; Luke got number 3 (pepper next to it for spicy), because he always ate crabs with extra hot sauce on the Chesapeake. He had on a Washington Nationals baseball cap. It reminded me of Jean Toomer, whose upbringing in the District of Columbia had shaped one of the great works of Modernist literature. Had it not been for that book, I would never have chosen to start writing that damned novel. The soups arrived. Matt, with two noodles drooping from the side of his lips, began barking, so other patrons turned to look at us. Jimmy slammed a glass bottle on the plastic place mat designed to look like bamboo. His eyes were beginning to glass over. Each young man drank the whiskey as the bowls of soup came out, except for Matt. He put his pinkies at the outside of his eyes, flattening them to tight ovals while staring at the Vietnamese woman who was serving our food, which caused me to drink more. I stood up abruptly and left, feeling as if I were floating. I saw myself flying, spreading giant wings, and appearing at Delilah's door, so drunk that she put me to bed. The dream played out in my brain: *Brooklyn's Eastern Parkway is deserted. It is the night. I begin to walk, and as I do, an Army recruitment office, a bank, and a fast-food restaurant pass on a conveyor belt to my left. I stare forward at the saplings on the Parkway, still bare. The night extends through the lenses of lightbulbs, twenty feet apart and dangling from silver fingers that protrude from beneath the tarred concrete. As I look into the tinted windows of a police car, the tip of my cigarette appears like a tiny furnace. All around there is a ringing.* It was 4:30 a.m. I tried to sleep, although I was nervous that the nightmares from last year were beginning again.

I woke up with an erection and someone's used bath towel on my face in the living room of the Rib Shack. I rinsed my mouth out with soap and water, and checked my eyes in the bathroom mirror before leaving the house. The mornings had become significantly colder than the afternoons, and I knew I was not prepared for winter. On the way up Pearl Street, I heard chanting from one block over. I turned to get closer to the noise and saw the outline of a husky bearded man with giant black headphones on, steadily rapping while thrusting his hands into the air. I watched him become small in the distance. At the cafeteria behind Billings Hall, there was a giant cardboard trifold headed with the word *Sodexo*. All of the options—the fresh greens, carrots, meats all salmonella-free—littered the blue background of the foldout. The lunch attendant stood in front of the display, with her burgundy uniform and black paper hat, waiting to swipe students' dining cards so they could ingest tons of processed American beef. The cafeteria was filled with light. The ceiling was Plexiglas and divided into eight raised panels that formed an octagonal pyramid. Though the windows at floor level were foggy with years of halfhearted maintenance, I sat next to them, facing a path and a small green. Outside, I saw Jimmy walking with Delilah. They were talking and smiling. He put his hand around her waist. As they disappeared from my periphery and I craned my neck to watch them, I had the sudden urge to walk in the opposite direction. I left the tray on the table and went toward Old Mill (1825, 1882), bypassing the Annex (1995) and the extension of the Royall Tyler Theatre (1915) while reading the architecture page to turn my brain from what it had just seen. None was designed before 1802— eleven years after the school's founding, when the institution had been more a high school for the children of wealthy Vermont landowners than a university. As I was looking at the dates of buildings, the novelty of American history became apparent, so I tried to find out what had occurred during the year of each building's construction. In 1825, the first American fraternity was founded; in 1882, New York was lit by electricity; in 1915, the United States reestablished diplomatic relations with Mexico; in 1995, Mississippi ratified the Thirteenth Amendment, becoming the last state to outlaw slavery.

None of the events seemed to be related. I arrived at my dorm room and the lights were out. Nothing was on Gary's side, and his bed had been stripped of its sheets. My eyes shut.

OCTOBER 18, 2010

I lay in bed and gazed out the window. The earth felt as if it were waiting. For what, I did not know. There were two students walking in different directions, next to the green. They smiled at each other. I could not hear their conversation, but their hand movements seemed to indicate that they would meet again, later that night. I got out of bed for the first time all day.

On the steps of the library, there was a man with sunglasses on, though it was dark. "I am the reckoning," he said. "I am the Lord of Light, and through me, all things are made small." He drank from the cup in his hand and projected again: "I am the Lord of Change." Most students walked by him; a few listened and chuckled with their friends. "I am the Lord and before me all things are infinitesimal." I faced the statue that resembled a dead and mutilated tree and walked on, trying not to be taken in by his madness.

Between Cook Physical Sciences and Wills Hall two seven-foot figures in black cloaks marched toward me. I stopped, realizing they were sculptures, then looked past them to the brick faces of the central campus dorms. Three cop cruisers were parked between Buckham and Chittenden (McKim, Mead & White). A small woman with brown hair cried in a blond man's arms just forty yards from me. Students bunched in groups outside the dorm. I did not wish to involve myself in the misfortune of others, so I continued to press forward, passing the Fleming

Museum (McKim, Mead & White). My eyes rested on the three sculptures that appeared to be pyramids, just before the entrance. Moving to their right, that angle changing my perception

of the shapes, I could see that the smallest installation was not a pyramid but half of a pointed oval, the flat side of which was on the ground. A raised spine ran down the center of it, affecting the same shape as the other two structures at certain vantage points. The day was haunted. I turned downtown and the police lights did not stop flashing until I crossed onto University Place. My nose was beginning to run. I knocked hard at Delilah's front door.

"Hello?" She had on a red sweater; the hood was drawn up, and there were bags under her eyes. I kissed her, pressing the mucus beneath my nostrils into her face, touching her ears with my hands. She withdrew. "You're cold."

"Can I come in?" Delilah left the door open and glided back into her room. She lay down on the bed and grabbed the glass of red wine she had been drinking, opening her computer again to watch an episode of *Law & Order*. I unfastened my jeans and closed her laptop. I asked, "Who is he?" We both knew that I was referring to Jimmy.

"What?"

"Tell me who he is," I said, as I wiped my nose and started to pull the sweater from her warm body.

"No." She turned over with her bra still on. I fussed with the straps; she slapped at my hands.

"I'm tired of slipping in between the mattress and the floor. At least sleep over in my room one time."

"I can't."

"You won't, or you can't?"

"I don't want to."

"Why?"

"You live in the dorms."

"Well, sleep with me over at the Rib Shack."

"That's not your house." She moved to the other side of the bed.

"I have a room there." I didn't reach for her.

She shrugged, opened the laptop, went to the bathroom, and turned on the water. I waited at the edge of the bed. She came out, hair in pins, and then walked to the kitchen, returning with more wine. Her left hand was on my stomach; my right hand was between her legs. I found myself staring around Delilah's room before dawn, taking the little things I saw in the night as some indication of who Delilah was. There was the dream catcher and an electronic gramophone with a record by the Funky Meters on top of it. There was a poster above her bed of an American football player wearing a University of Southern California Trojans jersey. On the adjacent wall there was a helmet, and pink goggles that hung above boots. A green snowboard rested beneath them. How did she learn to snowboard in the south? There were little things that I did not know about her, which made me realize that I had not taken a serious interest in Delilah. I tried to remember more of what she had told me about herself, but was distracted by the thought of a story Jean Toomer had written in *Cane*, called "Blood Burning Moon," about a black man (Tom) who killed a white man (Bob) over his continued dalliance with a young black woman (Louisa) whom Tom hoped to marry. It ended with Tom's hanging by lynch mob. What gave the story life were the horrible questions that went unasked by the narrator. Why had Louisa chosen to continue seeing Bob, why wasn't Tom given a fair trial, what did Tom truly desire? I linked that story to my life, Bob to Jimmy, though I knew it was absurd to see connections because the stories were separated by eighty-seven years (2010–1923) and reality. I turned over, propped up on my elbow, stared at Delilah's back and the light from her window. Behind the glass, standing on the corner of Pearl Street and South Union, reading a newspaper, was the man in the gray suit. He cast his eyes down, an action I could perceive although we were a great distance from each other. Delilah grunted, so I sat still, propped up like that, until the man returned my stare. He made a gesture toward the paper, closed it, then—

"How long have you been staring at me?" Delilah interrupted.

"I haven't been staring at you."

"David, I can see your reflection in the window." I tried to catch her eyes in the pane, but I could not. "Maybe you should go."

"Why?"

"You are acting weird."

Until then, I had not realized this night was Delilah's goodbye. I got out of the bed and started putting on my things. She went to sleep again. I turned the bottom lock on the front door. Soon I was facing due east, staring straight up Main Street. The sun began to rise. Night became dawn. Little birds began to tweet. It reminded me of the time I went to Melody's school with the letter. Now I turned right, into the athletic campus, and stopped between two dorms. No one was outside, so I sat in the little amphitheater between Millis and Austin Halls, twenty yards from the footpath, and stared out at the Green Mountains of Vermont.

Chapter 2

My legs were starting to stretch out. My knees and ankles ached some mornings. As I rubbed my joints for twenty minutes I stared at the fly netting that covered up the holes in the screen—sometimes pushing in, so it hurt, calming the pain with words. I touched the notebook Aunt Doris had gotten me. On the first two pages, I had written down some facts about the genius novelist Jean Toomer, separated by dashes. There was a brief biography of his life before the publication of Cane. "Looked white—Born 1894 though no record exists—Plessy v. Ferguson 1896—Grandson of P. B. S. Pinchback, governor of Louisiana, black, reconstruction, moved to Washington, D.C.—Father left— Moved to New Rochelle 1906—attended five different colleges 1915–1919—Cane published 1923." Two more entries followed the list: information written on June 9, 2006, that was about sand crabs; the other on December 8, 2006, that resembled a frantic apology on Orwell's 1984.

The act of journaling bothered me. When was the present? I couldn't carry the notebook around and write things as they happened. I had an idea to go back and re-create the past a month, two months after the fact, but when the date would come to write, I could not remember what, of significance, had transpired in those earlier days. I put the journal in the dresser beneath my socks and walked to the kitchen, where my aunt had already prepared breakfast. "What are you doing today?"

"Hanging out with Meat." I sat at the table.

"Always with that damned Meat."

"He's my only friend here."

"You don't need friends if that is the only one you could find."

"Why do you hate Meat?"

"He's vulgar."

"All the boys I know are vulgar."

"So what about girls?"

"What about them?" At this point, I was shoveling the eggs into my mouth.

"Why can't you be friends with a girl?"

"Do I look gay to you?"

"Any man who is friends with women is gay? That sounds backward to me."

"You don't get it."

"I don't. I was never a teenager."

"Is that sarcasm?"

"No."

I stared at her back, which had become more hunched over the years, and bit down on my fork by accident, which sent a ringing through my jaw. I tempered my condescension. "Thank you for breakfast."

"You are welcome." I left the house.

Meat and I moved past the green fields where the community band played concerts every Tuesday night in the summertime. He lit the joint from his sock. We coughed and made sure to keep the ember below our waists for a while before laying out the carnival plan. "If you want to fuck before high school ends," he said, "stick to the carnival plan. No girls from Montauk. No girls with younger sisters. No girls we already know. No girls that are friends of girls we already know." The rules were too time-consuming for me, plus I was waiting to mature, I thought, while pretending to pursue the only real ritual for young men in America—not school or Confirmation or Bar Mitzvah, but the loss of virginity. I had dreams that my penis had split down the middle; it bled out in a thick puddle of maroon. Five years ago, we were in Meat's living room playing video games at three in the morning when his older brother came downstairs and turned to Black Entertainment Television. "Watch this." The men paraded around the screen with the newest cars, watches, and pretty ladies. One man pulled out credit cards and slid them into the crease at the base of women's spines. Meat said, "If these niggas could guarantee me this shit in heaven, I'd blow up the fucking White House." We arrived at the mouth of the public beach and walked past the hard stares of white men in fluorescent security vests.

Most of the kids were vacationers. You could tell by the clothes they had on. The sneakers were too clean, the swim trunks too new. Part of their vacation was the acquisition of new things to bring on their vacation. Meat separated from me. I stopped by the Graviton and my eyes fixated on the red-and-purple machine as it sparkled and whirred around in a loop until the edges got blurry. "Dave!" By the fried dough truck, Meat called out to me, with his left hand hugging the flesh of a girl we knew. Talking to her was against the rules, but, as I saw him smiling, I realized there were no rules. Meat had laid out the "carnival plan" as a game; now he was acting on the will to quench the simplest desires, a frequent occurrence in adolescence. I walked toward them, stopping first at the fried dough truck for a funnel cake, before deciding not to enjoy their company. "Dave!" Meat shouted. I put two fingers to my lips, then turned away from him.

An alarm went off. I spilled some powdered sugar on my left pant leg. Looking down into the dead grass and straw wrappers, I saw a small red-and-white basketball shoe—spotless, barely touching the ground. My eyes traveled up the leg to a figure sitting on a stool and the face of a girl about my age. As your lips moved, the frown didn't lift from your brow. "Are you going to eat that?"

"This?" I pointed down at my funnel cake.

"Yeah."

"Most of it."

"Can I have a piece? What's your name?"

"David."

"Hello, David." You bit into the hardening cake. "So, do you live here?"

"No."

"I saw you talking to those kids, so I thought you did."

"No. My aunt lives here."

"Where do you live?"

"Harlem, with my mother."

"I'm from the city, too."

"Where?"

"Midtown."

"Where are you staying?"

You paused. "I'm just visiting my father's friend." I could not find my words, so you said, "I go to the Fieldston School. Do you know it?"

I shook my head and asked, "What are you doing tonight?"

"I have to be back at seven thirty."

"Can we hang out tomorrow?"

"I'm leaving."

"Oh." I shuffled my feet and could not find a way to move the conversation forward.

"That's it? Don't you want my number?"

I dusted off the cardboard plate and handed it to you, clutching the last piece of cake. Your handwriting was not curly; each line bumped into the next, making hard stops at the end of consonants. "MELODY." I put the cake on the plate again and left the carnival, passing the five safety patrolmen in orange, feeling nauseated, and headed in the direction of my house. Shit. I ran back to the water drain on Bay Street and tried to fish out the paper plate with those nine numbers etched onto it. I couldn't reach the ruffled edges. I searched my mind for the figures, 917-9(blank)31, but could not remember them. I turned and searched the carnival. You were nowhere to be found.

What bothered me about what I had written was that I had borrowed so freely from my experience to produce the characters. The changes that I did make were small. Aunt Doris is my real mother, I had not thrown away Melody's plate, but had waited—as the days went by, I became too nervous to call her. In truth, I was devising a way to keep up the lie I told about my mother living in Harlem. Still, I did not know what drove me to make the protagonist lie as well.

Why I had chosen to write like this, so self-consciously, was probably due to a misreading of *Cane*, I thought. I assumed Toomer had created so many characters in his work as a way to distract the reader from his inability to sustain one narrative, but maybe that was not the case. I was then shaken by the realization that literary genius was the ability to create strong, original characters, and my main character was myself. I should think about going to the student health clinic, I thought. I said to myself, "You should mull over going to the student health clinic," just to hear it out loud. How do you control your mind? Rather, how do you force your brain to stop remembering? The questions remained unanswered, so I returned to the living room of the Rib Shack and drank my ninth shot of whiskey. Jimmy kept looking at me and grinning, though I chose not to engage him. Then I was vomiting; then there was a tab of lysergic acid diethylamide in the beer I was drinking; then I was out in a meadow next to Centennial Baseball field for the first time, with my ear to a large oak tree; then I was running behind Chittenden dorm—

Me: How have you been, Melody? 2:13 a.m.
Me: I'm lost without you. 2:16 a.m.

I threw the phone back in my jacket pocket, zipped it all the way up to my neck, and caught some skin in the metal contraption just below my Adam's apple. I walked right, down Colchester Avenue. I began to jog as the road descended, winding left at the bottom of the hill. Finding myself at some point on the bank of the Winooski River, which seemed to be miles from where I had come, I went to sleep on a bench, too disoriented to trek back uphill.

I woke up with my hood over my head and my feet curled up beneath my butt. The tree in front of me had two placards nailed to it, one labeled "Closed to Fishing (March 16–May 31)." The other had a painting of an endangered lake sturgeon and begged you to release the fish if caught. I stretched my arms and legs, turning to see the sign "Salmon Hole (0.2 Miles to Path)" before looking back to the river, where the man in the gray suit was standing by the bank. The sheen of water that moistened the marsh appeared in a trinity of shallow pools. He stared at me, then started spreading the riverbank on his face. I turned back to the road. I could not feel my fingers or toes, which would have worried me had I strayed as far from campus as I had assumed last night. The sun was bright. I walked uphill, past a graveyard with a tall statue of a man on a pillar raising his left hand next to an obelisk. The path bent, and I headed northwest toward the dorms before the sight of a building with a golden orb above its belfry caused me to stop again. This chapel had been constructed by McKim, Meade & White, just like Southwick Music Hall on Redstone Campus, which had prompted me to start researching campus architecture. None of the buildings designed by the firm had been erected before its founder Stanford White was killed.

Now that I was thinking clearly, it seemed obvious that the architecture and the man in the gray suit were pointing me toward some truth. The aphorism "reach back and get it" came to my mind. It meant to take the best of the past and bring it into the present. I was not heeding this advice. There was the sound of a car's horn. I turned around and saw that I had been holding up traffic while staring at the building from the middle of the street. My mouth, like an oven of lies and deceit, spoke to itself, as the grease of intoxicants animated my legs. Move forward.

I am walking with a group of students, but I am not myself. We move down rows of naked saplings, some of which had been uprooted in a storm last November. A path lights up in front of me. In the near distance is the university's furnace. It is engulfed by flames. I crouch, put my fingers on the chalked outline of a cross that is adorned with a heart and bloodied human ribs. All around there is a humming. It reaches a deafening volume. I look up to the fire and find thousands of students, their arms spread out, ascending.

I woke up drenched in sweat, remembering the barest hints of the dream. My voice was saying "prescience." The word, meaning foreknowledge, was linked to some painting I had walked by with Melody, and a scene that had yet to occur. I could feel a presence in the room. I did not open my eyes. I felt him hovering over me, staring into my dream. His mouth was ajar, bearing a white grin, as if each tooth was a joke he was dangling above my head. "It is cynical," I thought. "His grin is cynical."

I dressed without using the bathroom and rushed to the Davis Center to look for the school's newspapers. I pushed past students who were eating, interrupted then upset, and collected Issue 9, November 2, 2010. Page 1 read, "Student Found Dead in Chittenden Hall on October 18," and I realized that had transpired on the last day I visited Delilah's house. On page 7, there was another article about a young man's demise, "Loss Felt Throughout UVM Community," which occurred earlier in October. The whole issue conformed to a narrative: youth and death. There was something horrifying and reductive about the way we memorialized the deceased. I continued to turn the pages to a headline that read, "Students Gather for a Marathon of Writing."

The wait for the psychologist was seven minutes. It had taken three days to get an appointment through the school's website. I woke up to the sight of snow flurries and got dressed, putting on a blue-and-red tie before picking my hair out so that the dense curls became an afro. I felt like a child going to his first day of school.

"I'm Dr. Amelia."

"Nice to meet you."

"Can you tell me why you came in today?"

I felt like a boy in a man's body. "I need help."

"That is a brave thing to say."

"I have not been myself lately." I looked at the wall behind her; there was a purple flag with a golden wheel in the center pinned to it. "In the preference column I wrote female, and I hope that does not offend you."

"Should it?"

"My mother is also a psychologist, of sorts, so I thought it would be more comfortable." Scribble, scribble, scribble.

"Where did she practice?"

"In the living room."

"While you were there?" I tried to redirect her attention. I gave a road map of my life, making sure to omit mention of the man in the gray suit. I talked about my mother in Long Island, feeling alone, and Jean Toomer, ending with Melody. She wrote something down, then removed her glasses and spoke frankly about this being her first job. I told her I hated everyone, hated this session, and hated her compliance, which did not abate until I was empty of thirty-six minutes of talk.

"Have you ever thought it's not your mother you dislike but your father?"

"No."

"Why isn't your father in any of the stories?"

"Because he wasn't there."

"But not at all? That's a little strange, don't you think?"

"I did have a couple of dreams about him."

"And?"

"My mother is crazy."

"Is there no empathy for people who suffer from mental illness?"

"You're twisting my words. I didn't say she was mentally ill."

"Sorry. You said crazy."

"I meant crazy like black crazy, you know, she's crazy." Amelia wrote that down. She moved on.

"Has there been any significant change in your schedule since you left home?"

"No."

"Did you work out before, play an instrument before coming to college?"

"No."

"Do you have any hobbies or—?"

"I was trying to write a novel."

"Have you tried to submit to the school literary journal?"

"It's not finished."

"Do you want to finish it?"

"I don't think so."

"If the mood strikes you to write, try. If it is making you stressed, then stop." I assured her I would follow this advice, and she sent me to the medical offices across campus, to have an appointment with Dr. Hume.

The building was a quarter of a mile away, so I opened the Internet browser and searched for "Vermont, medicine, psychology, tests," stumbling upon a narrative I had not read before. The page heading was a picture of green mountains, interrupted by straw huts and a leafless white tree. The portal told the story of eugenics at the university, starting with Professor Henry F. Perkins, director of the Department of Zoology. In the photograph, dated 1928, he was clean-shaven and his mouth was turned down. Though confidence was depicted in this pose, the receding hairline, the small left eye—little imperfections—seemed to hint at the mania that led to his descent into alcoholism. He had spent his life trying to weed this and other diseases from the genetic pool. I entered www.uvm.edu/~eugenics/partnersf.html and read the report of the Academic Advisory Committee, which presided over the Vermont Eugenics Survey. The study targeted those with the traits of mental illness called Huntington's chorea. They included the pirate families of Vermont (French Canadians living in houseboats on Lake Champlain) and the Gypsies (those with dark skin because of African or Abenaki Native American blood). Between the years 1933 and 1938, 131 sterilizations took place. This number is skewed, as are most American surveys of the time, because the state did not keep proper records of the Native American population. As I looked to the Internet, under images of the Abenaki tribe, I saw many descendants who had strong European roots. As I tried to do more research on eugenics and Native Americans, the information became harder to find.

Dr. Hume shook my hand and asked me some questions, before deciding: "Twenty-milligram tablets of citalopram." I went to the pharmacy on the floor above the doctor's office to fill my scrip before braving the flurries and returning to the dorm just in time to see three young men at the end of my hall get arrested. Two cops passed me without a word. I felt removed from the present. I entered my room and sat on my bed. Time passed as I looked out the window at the night sky. I rolled a joint and sat smoking by the fan, with the orange plastic container in my hand. The floor was beginning to collect pizza boxes and old newspapers. From the bedside, I picked up my notebook, placing it in the trash. I closed the blinds and shut off the lights, then lay on the bed in darkness. My eyelids began to sink, though my mind kept my body from falling into sleep. Between here and there I saw a wound, big and pink, with veins and blood, which I could crawl into. I wanted to lock myself inside and heal until I was new, but time continued forward, and on and on and on.

Act
II

Melody had given herself a haircut. "Take a picture of me." The thick curls stopped near the middle of her neck. They stood in contrast to the black tuft on my head, which was behind the lens of an instant film Polaroid camera. We were on the West Side Highway, passing the new bike lane, avoiding each other's eyes. I stole glances. Everything fought on her face, from her full mouth to her narrow eyes, her straight teeth to her crooked teeth. As we began moving again, the sound of a thousand bumblebees followed us through the sky, which was clear. She asked, "Do you hear that humming?" I nodded. Planes crossed high above. My eye caught the construction that would become One World Trade Center. It was designed to appear as two buildings wrapped in one. Each would be four-sided, triangular, though one stretched down and the other up, as if they had resurrected the two older towers and combined them. Now it was just loud banging and a rust-colored frame. I continued to pan. A yellow sailboat with white masts pulled into the harbor. Melody's eyes followed as it docked. We walked out on the stone jetty and sat facing New Jersey. She liked to sit in quiet, I in discovery. The Colgate sign illuminated the Jersey City shoreline. We were staring at the horizon, watching a ferry leave for Staten Island, when I placed my hand on hers. We sat like that, occasionally parting to wipe sweat from our faces. I thought I would be more nervous—that somehow I would stumble and she would discover that I did not live in Harlem. This fear excited me, and any hesitation I may have had about

seeing her subsided. I turned back to her face and she was smiling, still looking at the horizon.

After an hour or so, I stood and apologized for having to
leave so soon. She hugged me and then walked east toward the
center of the financial district, though she lived on the west side.
I stayed behind her at a distance and crossed onto Vesey Street,
watching the pink soles of her sneakers, her awkward gait, until
Church Street, where she turned right. The word *voyeur* popped
into my head. I stared up at St. Paul's Chapel, which had served
as a base for rescue workers after September 11, 2001, and let her
disappear around the corner of an office building. I entered the
2/3 subway station at Park Place, and took the train to Four-
teenth Street, transferring back to the 1 train to Canal Street,
where I got off and walked up Varick, making a right on Broome
Street, arriving in the classroom at 5:07 p.m.

I had taken the Beginner class at Daily Planet Writer's Workshop in the fall, the Building class in the spring. Jim had been my
teacher last semester, and was this one as well. His mother
founded the program, so he knew the lesson plans well and interpreted them liberally. He had practical advice: "This is how
to brainstorm, this is how to be more consistent with your writing, this is how to link one idea to the next using prepositions
but avoiding prepositional phrases, here is a gramophone [he
drew] and here is a phonogram [he wrote]," or, "This is Chek-
hov's device [he chalked a rifle]. Always write like this. If you
begin the story with a gun, make sure it is used before the end
of the final act. This is a red herring [he drew a fish with smoke
rising from it]. Never write like this. If someone is smoking a
herring in the background, make sure there is a reason you have
included that detail in your story." When it came to the act of
creating—the what—he would say, "Write about something you

know well so you can give us details an outsider would take years to learn."

As I read the syllabus, I noticed the first five thousand words of our novels were not due until the middle of October, and we did not finish the manuscripts at tier three, but at tier four, after which they gave us the certificate that proved we were novelists. The first assignment was to go to the library and read books of poetry—it would help us with dialogue. Jim presented the information with a devious smile, so we would think he had invented this trick. I tried to pay attention but Melody's silhouette kept coming to my mind. Next week, I would have to get the bus earlier so as to spend more of the day with her. I calculated: bus 7:30 a.m., arrive 10:30, Melody's apartment 11:00. How long would she enjoy these Saturday visits before she became curious about what I did with the rest of my week? All of that seemed far in the future, so I focused back on the lesson plan and tried to absorb more of Jim's teaching.

Chapter 3

*I woke up on March 28 and Doris was in my room singing.
"Happy Birthday to you" rang out over and over again. I realized
the power of the song was in its repetition.*

"Are you all right?" I asked.

*"I'm fine." There was a manila envelope on the kitchen
counter with my name on it. "That is for you." I opened the envelope to a card, which had a bear telling a donkey, "I would
wish you a happy birthday . . ." The inner flap read, ". . . but I
know you find this holiday unBEARable." It had sixty dollars in
it and a small journal. I hugged her. The erection that followed
a night of rest was shrinking, but still swollen enough to cause
a moment of discomfort between us. I went back to my room
and got dressed before heading to the front door.*

"Where are you going?"

"To hang out." I closed the door before she could object.

The path sloped down toward the center of town. I turned right, into the cove before the public beach. There was a patch of grass in front of me where the carnival was hosted annually. Two robins were foraging for worms. As my body approached, they floated away, squawking to the nearest tree. I continued down the paved roadway until I reached the wooden gate that separated the town from the bay. There was a white pickup truck in the parking lot next to small bushels of sea grass, stalks of sea oats. I sat on the thick wooden fence and looked beyond the silver slide and the teenagers from my school I pretended not to know. Small waves marbled then crashed. The light blue sky was interrupted by white clouds. I left the beach.

I was thinking of a book my English teacher had assigned us: Travels with Charley by John Steinbeck. The book began with the protagonist (Steinbeck) leaving Sag Harbor (this town) with his deceased wife's poodle, to drive across America, a country he had written so much about but had not traveled around in twenty-five years. I walked through the center of town, as I knew Steinbeck had, and made my way to the John Jermain Memorial Library to finish reading his book. It was a mass of wooden shelves and hard wooden chairs. The librarian was new, though she resembled the old librarian. I thought to ask for Travels with Charley but was embarrassed by the inferences she would make about my taste, so I tried to imagine a serious book of fiction, written by a black author, though nothing came to mind.

"I'm looking for the Harlem Renaissance books," I said.

"Were you thinking of a specific work?"

"No."

"I'm sure we have a copy of Cane here. Do you want to see that one?"

I nodded. She took me down one of the rows and went looking through each shelf. We stopped at what seemed to be in the geometric center of the library. Cane *was bound in green and gold painted leather. The image on the front was pastoral, and I didn't understand most of the sentence — neither "Her skin is like dusk on the eastern horizon . . ." nor "Black reapers with the sound of steel on stones are sharpening scythes." As the librarian returned to her desk, I asked, "I thought this was a novel?"*

"It is."

"But there are a bunch of poems in it."

"Well, that is a part of the novel." She continued along her way. I propped myself against the shelf, reading until I became light-headed. On page 63, there began a section called "Theater," which featured a character named Dorris. Seeing a name so similar to my aunt's in a book I opened at random was like a sign from God. I wondered if anyone else could enjoy the story like I could. I continued through it, too lazy to get a dictionary, memorizing the words: "Cassava, hone, palabra, profligate, vesper," repeating them as if they were an incantation. I waited for the librarian to return from the bathroom. "May I check the book out?"

The clouds made no distinct shapes. From the top of Doris's street, I saw the florist's car outside. The garage was not open, which was abnormal. I stubbed my foot on the front steps, and the nail of my right big toe felt as if it was beginning to come off. I ran into the bathroom for the peroxide and a Band-Aid, and the house was unusually quiet. Curiosity overtook me. I walked down the hallway, across from my room, and put my ear to Doris's door. I heard her moaning, like after a wheeze, or when she sat on the toilet late at night, but this moan was deeper — like she was reaching out. I opened the door; Jeff, the florist, jumped into the closet.

When the sheets settled, she was staring at me, grinning. "Did you want to see this, you little nasty— " I closed the door and went to the beach before she could finish her phrase.

The clouds were still nondescript. Doris came to pick me up. I looked at my hands and saw Cane, which I hadn't released since leaving the library. It was like the book had directed me to this truth about Doris. The Band-Aid was collecting sand. The bay was calm; sailboats bobbed in the green breeze. The horn beeped four times, but I didn't go to the car. I wanted to get far away from this small town, but at fourteen, the farthest I could go was inside a book. I sat in the shallows of the bay and began to read the final chapter, entitled "Kabnis," paying closer attention to detail.

I called Melody on Friday and asked if we could see each other but she was busy with something, she said—her father was going on a trip, and she wanted to be with him before he left. She asked me to come over on Sunday, but I told her there was no way, so we agreed to see each other next weekend. I had to go to the city early Saturday morning, anyway, because I had already lied to my mother.

The bus dropped me off at Fortieth and Third. I walked to Grand Central and took the S train before transferring to the C at Times Square going north. I exited on 135th Street and walked uphill across a park, paying scant attention to the green, and arrived at the east gate of City College, my mother's alma mater. I had memorized the route from here to the closest public library, on 125th Street, so I could finish my homework for the workshop. I walked down St. Nicholas Terrace, passing young white and brown people, not three blocks south from where the campus ended. I crossed 127th Street and counted the building numbers—356, 358, 360—and stopped at 362, where my mother had raised me for five years. Curious, I thought, that it was so close to her former university, and, of the ten or so identical apartment buildings on 127th Street between St. Nicholas Terrace and Convent Avenue, it was the only one that had been destroyed by fire. Earlier that week I had taken a book from my mother's shelf entitled *Harlem: Two Centuries of Architecture*, because I wanted to learn more about the neighborhood in case Melody happened to ask me any questions. The place had been settled by the Dutch first, then became an enclave of working-class Jewish and Italian immigrants, who gave way to other peoples with histories of being colonized, starting in the 1900s. By the 1930s, Harlem was 70 percent black. I was not sure if this information would be useful. At the corner of 125th Street and Morningside Avenue, a Puerto Rican man came rolling by. He mumbled something unintelligible. I looked to his dry lips, with small bubbles of spit, to his shoes, wing-tipped and spotless, with the desire to wash his feet. The ecstasy was fleeting, and I left the interaction with a vague idea of my emotions as patronizing and out of touch. I felt there was some disconnect between the history I had learned and the people I now saw.

I entered the George Bruce branch of the New York Public Library. It reminded me of the John Jermain library in Sag Harbor, which was built in 1910, and I wondered if the similarities were due to their both being public libraries or to a greater trend in early twentieth-century American architectural design. I strolled down the poetry aisle and picked up *The Cantos of Ezra Pound*, because it was orange and reminded me of *The Count of Monte Christo* as I said it fast. I opened to the day of my birth. Page 28, Canto VIII, read:

> These fragments you have shelved (shored).
> "Slut!" "Bitch!" Truth and Calliope
> Slanging each other sous les lauriers:
> *That* Alessandro was negroid . . .

The rest of the poem bored me. Next to *The Cantos* there was a maroon book, with a middle-aged black man in a newsboy hat and gray suit on the cover, holding flowers close to his chest. The book was some combination of photography and poetry, based on Langston Hughes and Roy DeCarava's *Sweet Flypaper of Life*. I found myself assaulted with colloquial mannerisms—"Hey brothah, what happened"—which I didn't like, even when they appeared in *Cane*. I skimmed to the middle of the book, stopping at the picture of a solitary black boy, sitting on his heels while staring west on 125th Street. Adults gathered at the entrance to the Harlem State Office Building. I felt the picture was missing something. I put the book down and walked to the computer. I typed "State Office Building Harlem" into the browser, viewing the images tab, finding the same office as in the picture. If I had guessed the date correctly by the style of clothes, it was the re-naming ceremony for the Adam Clayton Powell Jr. Building, an event that occurred in 1983. Had the picture in the book been captured after the year 2005, I thought, the photographer would have been standing against the statue of Adam Clayton Powell, Jr., which held three golden bubbles against its base. They read "Keep," "the," and "Faith." It stated neither to whom nor in what.

I passed the statue of Christopher Columbus at Columbus Circle and stopped across the street from a pharmacy and a luxury hotel. I looked at a gray sculpture, cut to resemble two humans in seated positions, outside Melody's apartment building. The entrance was on the south side of the street. As I spun into the lobby, the doorman was blocking the entrance, his face uncomfortably close to my face.

"Which apartment?"

"Richard Gilbert."

"I'm sorry, he is not in."

"Melody told me to come over."

"Hold on." He walked back to his stand, mumbled something into a telephone, then waved me on—"Forty-three c."

"Thank you."

The elevator doors opened, and I turned right, pushing the small gray button next to the eyehole of the apartment. Melody's footsteps echoed into the hallway.

"Hey."

"Hey." There was an awkward silence.

"Beautiful," I said.

"Shut up."

The artwork on the walls was sparse. Melody's father had moved in five years prior, but the furniture was left over from the showing. They had boxes of paintings and posters, but nothing from the Lower East Side, where they used to live, had made it to the walls of the Upper West Side home.

"Nice place."

"We haven't settled in."

"I can tell."

"I don't know if he wants to stay."

"Why did you move?"

"Something about his father's spirit and this neighborhood . . . I don't listen to him when he talks about his father." I stood over by one of the windows looking out on Central Park. "He gets back next month. Do you want to meet him?"

"Not really."

"I don't blame you," she said, then walked into the kitchen to heat up a Cup o' Noodles. "He doesn't like to hang things on the wall." When I roamed to her bedroom, it became apparent she did not either. There was an easel in the corner, and a white dresser with a framed picture on it. A woman in a swimsuit stared down the lens of a camera; her legs, crossed at the ankles, shifted her weight, and one hip seemed to curve up in a smirk. Her hair was '80s big. On the wall next to her bed, Melody had painted sketches of birds: parrots, doves, finches, and hawks, in different primary colors that descended into the point of a triangle.

"It's like cave paintings," she said, entering the room with noodles in her mouth.

"This is a high cave."

"That's why I painted so many birds." And they were composed with great attention to detail.

"Do you want to be a painter?"

"That sounds so simple. I am having fun exploring art right now. I don't know if it is evocative to others yet, but I don't care either." She put the foam cup next to a picture frame on her desk.

"But are you going to do it in college?"

"I haven't decided yet. How about you?"

"What do you mean?"

"Are you going to continue to write in college?"

"I think so." Her eyes began to crease; her cheeks rose, baring a sliver of teeth.

"You should try poetry."

"I don't like poetry."

"Rick's got a couple of poet friends. Literal couple. He says they are annoying, but they are the smartest people he brings here."

"Why do you call him Rick?"

"What else would I call him?"

"Father." She tilted her head. I crossed the wooden floor to her window and tried to look out to the east side.

"You're staring like you have never looked out a window before."

"I haven't looked out of one this high."

She touched my back. "What floor is your mother's apartment on?"

"Four." I turned to face her. "It's just funny to be this far from the ground."

She stood in front of me with her jean shorts down near her ankles, unfastening the straps of her bra. I closed the distance between us.

"Hold on." She drew the shades, placing a red T-shirt over the lamp beside her desk.

We were lying down together. I kissed and rubbed her stomach. The birds, now covered in red light, seemed less childish. She had painted all of their irises golden, which made them appear to be alive. I stared at her nipples, which were just below the beak of a green dove, the tip of the upside-down triangle, swooping low from the mass of other bodies. It was not just the sight of her nakedness that caused my arousal, but the fact that while she lay bare, I was still concealing myself. I began to laugh. My penis became more erect. I took off my clothes and kept trying to put myself inside her. She just smiled shyly and turned away. "Not yet." I checked the clock on her wall, 5:37 p.m., and decided to cut class. She hugged her breasts to my torso before pushing away to marvel at my skin. She grabbed it, pulling slowly, stretching my body flat with her other hand. When she put her thumb to my neck, I came. She let go, and as I started to get up, she said, "Don't move," then walked to her dresser and pulled out a camera. "I'm just going to take a picture of your stomach," she said, adding, "I promise," before standing over my legs with the lens pointed at my belly. I lay still and let her finish. Melody waved the image in the air, trying to quicken its development, then let it rest on the bed. The scale of the brown body and the three pools of liquid would have been inconceivable had I not been there for the creation of the picture. We stared at it in silence.

"I have to go," I said.

"Already? Can you come back tomorrow?"

"Tomorrow will be difficult."

"Why?"

"I have to make sure my mother takes her medication tonight."

"What's wrong with her?"

"I'd rather not talk about it. For now."

"But what's wrong with her?" I shook my head, and she stopped asking questions, realizing how forward she was being.

I said, "I feel—" before cutting myself off. I fixed my face again, held her shoulders in my palms, and we stood there for a while before I descended the elevator, and then the escalator that led to the train beneath Columbus Circle.

I crossed Morningside Avenue and passed Saint Joseph of the Holy Family Church, reading, "Daily Mass, 9:00 a.m. in English, 7:00 p.m. in Spanish." The building had bright red doors, and the bricks were red as well, though not as loud as the entrance. Beneath the belfry there was a golden-domed chamber facing the street. St. Joseph stood, holding the baby Jesus in his left hand and a scepter in his right. I daydreamed it was not Jesus but Jean Toomer in the chamber, and not Joseph, but Toomer's grandfather P. B. S. Pinchback. I walked across 125th Street, due west, toward the George Bruce branch of the New York Public Library. I didn't feel much like reading, poetry or fiction. I searched some bookshelves, in a very inefficient manner, for the late author's work, discovering what I had hoped to (nothing). Not sure what to do next, I sat at one of the public computers. My guidance counselor had given me a list of colleges to look through, most of which were part of the State University of New York system. I went on websites for SUNY this or SUNY that—pages that took too much time to load—then I looked at the schools he had listed as reaches, ones I might not have been focused enough to attend: Pepperdine University, Cal Berkeley, Oberlin, and Rice. The idea of being so far removed from my mother calmed me, then I became upset about what the distance would do to Melody and me. It was now 11:30, and I found myself looking at an encyclopedia article about Melody's father. "Richard 'Rick' Gilbert (né Richard Murzynowicz II) grew up on the Lower East Side of Manhattan. His father was a gynecologist, and his mother, Dorothy, was a schoolteacher. Richard Sr. was dismissive of his son's aspirations to be an artist. When he passed away in 1987, Rick did not attend his funeral." I skimmed some more passages, but the synopses became briefer as the late '80s turned to the early '90s. By the mid-'90s, the article had all but fizzled out. The last sentences read, "In 1994, Rick's girlfriend Magda passed away in their home from heart failure. This death, and the rearing of the couple's child, Melody Gilbert, made him retreat from the public sphere." I looked at the article's picture of Melody's father. He was smiling. There was stubble on his chin and circular green sunglasses covered half of his face. I typed "Rick Gilbert paintings" into the browser and found *The City's Forgotten*, Richard Gilbert, 1982, which was linked to www.metmuseum.org/. I tried to make sense of the brown and gray blotches, before closing out of the browser to meet Melody.

"Stolen," she kept repeating, "stolen." I looked down at the black circles that surrounded the obelisk from Heliopolis, Egypt, that was behind the Metropolitan Museum of Art. When I told her I had wanted to go to a downtown museum, she said that the only art worth the admission was Egyptian. At first, I found this connection to my mother and her interests as some sign to leave Melody, but as we walked through the jewelry of Sithathoryunet (ca. 19th Century B.C.E.) and the Temple of Dendur (1st Century B.C.E.) she kept repeating "stolen," loudly enough to disturb other patrons, as if she were a part of the exhibit, I knew that she and my mother did not share the same understanding of history. As I began telling Melody about the discrepancy between the naming of Cleopatra's Needle and the history of Ramses II, she became annoyed. "They had no right to name it in the first place."

"Who is they?"

"The English."

"Maybe we should go to a different exhibit, then."

"Wasn't that enough?"

"Let's expand."

"Oh, expansion, that's nice—"

"The American section?"

"Absolutely not."

"Just for a second." She made her eyes narrow, suspecting that I knew about her father's painting, but could not object without admitting to its existence. We walked up the museum steps, past the packs of bumbling tourists, toward the second floor. A security guard started to say something in our general direction, so I pulled out of my pocket the small pin that proved I had paid the suggested donation. Once above the grand staircase, we turned left and right, searching for the hallway devoted to our national artwork—past the eighteenth-century canvases, the fifth-century Byzantine stained glass, and many other marvels of the Christian world I did not fully register, because my eyes were focused on Melody's back. The yellow bag bobbed away, rubbing against her washed blue jeans, and the gray jacket hung around her waist. She glided in front of a painting entitled *Prescience*, and put her hair in a bun. A European man tried to stop his young daughter and son from fighting while a woman rolled her mother through the exhibit in a wheelchair. The older woman stared, eyes filled with nostalgia, as the younger one checked something on her cell phone. As we walked by *The City's Forgotten* by Richard Gilbert, she hurried to point out the next canvas, a painting called *Black Iris*.

I was captivated by the strokes at the top of the canvas. It was neither colorful nor big. White petals, on top of black petals—it was pink inside, with red lips.

"See something you like?"

"It's intense," I said.

"O'Keeffe."

"It has a certain depth—"

"It's just a pussy." She laughed. "You'll probably like this one too, then."

The white pearl balanced on a curve that started at the top right of the canvas and stopped at the bottom left. The pearl pulsated. Its gray rings rippled across the blackness. I began to sense what would come next. It would be raining on that late afternoon; drizzle would spot us as we got out of a cab that she would pay for, the droplets reminding me of the painting *Black Abstraction* by Georgia O'Keeffe. Her father would not be home, again. She would lie on the bed, perpendicular to its length, and I would put the condom on the wrong way twice, before the tip filled with air. I found it beautiful. As she spread her legs, I shut everything out—how I got here, whether my desire for Melody was true—and focused on the physical act. It was dramatic and quick; she sat against the wall, and I laid my head in her lap. I began to hum. "What are you doing?" she asked. "Humming, Melody." We laughed together. We tried again, I licked again, and the short sounds she emitted made me aroused again. I balanced between sleep and wakefulness, on the other side of my virginity, until dawn crept through the single window in Melody's room. And in the morning, she awoke slowly. Her hair was pressed against my shoulder. She began to tell me a story. "My mother grew up in Sonora, Mexico, and was discovered at fifteen." There was a picture of Magdalena from *Vogue* on Melody's dresser. "She passed away because her heart was too big. They did cocaine, Rick and she. Her heart was too big." I tried to affect surprise, though I'd read on the Internet of her mother's untimely death. In the end, Melody's eyes were sad, and I tried to console her.

Chapter 4

I had to cross Route 114 to get to my house from school. There were two blind curves—Doris always said, "Look both ways twice before you pass." I looked twice both ways, and a red pickup truck did not slow down at the curve. Two more cars had passed before I made it to Hempstead Street. I turned onto Richards Drive. The sky was so gray it seemed to be one sheet of cloud. Three crows had perched on the highest wire of the telephone pole that bisected Doris's house. They did not call. I walked to the door and slid the key inside. I went to the refrigerator, made a peanut-butter-and-jelly sandwich, and thought about turning the TV on, but I did not want to wake my aunt. I put the dishes in the sink, then tiptoed to my bedroom. I went to the window and looked at the crows, which turned from time to time to stare at me. Even they were silent for Doris.

Now I lay me down to sleep.
I pray the Lord, my soul to keep.

She was not home. I picked the lock with a butter knife and entered her room. The teal bedspread could have been from any decade after 1950. There were tan and white stripes on the wallpaper. Everything in the room was neat except the paintings she had hung. They were turned upside down seemingly at random. There were the idols: Sophia, Erzuli, and Isis. All three of them had been painted by the same artist. The room had three closets, one to the right of the door, which held her jackets and robes, another to the left, next to the television, which was stuffed with papers and boxes. In the third closet was an armoire that had been crafted into a bookshelf. It held books in languages I could not comprehend. There were two volumes called The Book of the Dead, *one from Tibet and one from Egypt, that came with translations.*

Once I asked Doris, "Who else speaks Hieroglyph?"

"People don't speak Hieroglyph. They wrote in hieroglyphs."

"What do they speak? Hieroglyphan?"

"No. The language that goes with the words doesn't exist anymore."

"That's confusing, Aunt Doris."

"I know it is."

"Why do you read it if no one speaks it?"

"Because there are important things you can only understand in their original forms, even if no one speaks the language anymore—but you have to be careful. Some of these books are powerful, and if you read them too young, they will destroy your brain forever."

"That isn't possible, Aunty."

She stepped back—"Yes, it is"—and looked at my face for confirmation.

"Behold Osiris!
Ani the scribe—who recordeth the holy offerings
of all the gods—who saith,
homage to thee who hast come as Khepera."

One night I awakened to the sound of a truck's motor. Doris was out front, speaking to the florist. He wore a camouflage baseball cap and was smiling, as she motioned for him to enter the driveway. The truck bed was filled with sodden earth. Doris opened the garage. Together, they began shoveling the dirt inside.

When he left and she came up to her room, she shouted, "Where are my books?"

"What—"

"Don't play with me."

I went to get the books from underneath my bed, but they had disappeared.

"Now apologize for lying."

"I am sorry."

"What did I tell you?"

"I can't understand them."

"Good, stop being so curious about things you are too young for." I nodded and turned to leave. "Put on a clean shirt, we have people coming over."

"Why do I always have to do what you want me to do?"

"Go to your room and change your T-shirt." I looked into her eyes. "Are you hard of hearing?" I stood still. "Listen, little nigger, I'm not arguing with you now, go change!" I went to my room. Since there was no lock on the door, I pushed my dresser in front of it. At 7:45, she came to get me. First, she knocked, then used force. I pressed my weight against the dresser. She kept managing to crack the door open, whispering threats into the wood. The doorbell tolled. She whispered, "I'll let you look at the books, just come out tonight."

"Are you sure?" I asked.

"Yes," she hissed. I opened the bedroom door. She motioned downstairs, toward the knock at the front, and reminded me to "say it right this time," her voice still in a whisper. I walked down the hallway, turned the locks, and said, "Welcome, Doris will be with you in a moment, she just saw a vision of the new millennium."

"And who are you?"

I responded, "Her nephew," then moved aside as the two white strangers stepped over the threshold, into the house.

We all sat in different places around the living room. Doris said, "My nephew is here to help you deal with your shame." I nodded at them.

The husband said, "I don't know."

Doris responded, "We should begin there. Why did you hesitate?"

He said, "I don't know."

"Good," she said. "Let us start with not knowing. A particular type of depression." The couple looked at each other, confused. Doris let the tension rise. Finally, she said, "Depression, the kind that can get you prescribed light dosages of selective serotonin reuptake inhibitors, is a code word for American guilt."

To which the wife said, "How did you know I was on antidepressants?"

Doris smiled and went to the closet to get two blankets. "We know these things." She motioned for both of her patients to lie down. They closed their eyes.

"You are sitting in your bedroom, holding hands, looking out to sea. You hear the wind from outside, and all of your concerns are so far away. Imagine yourself on the roof of your house, still looking out to the beach. You can smell the sea now." She waved to me, as the strangers had their eyes closed, so I would sit across from her and caress the bottoms of their feet. *"Now you are focusing because we have to build this journey together. You are in a boat, just the two of you. It is small, and the sea is vast. You look down to the right. Karen, what do you see?"*

And if I die before I wake?
I pray the Lord, my soul to take.

I am seated in front of a building with ten identical Grecian pillars. I cannot remember what it is that I am thinking about. There is a piercing cry to my right and I begin to sprint in the other direction. My feet stop, I blink, and all around me is blackness. A force pushes me back, sends me sliding toward the bottom of a curve until the tip of a giant talon punctures my sternum. As the life fades from my eyes, I look toward the horizon, which is opening to reveal a golden orb. All around, I feel a rumbling, and from the waters, the outlines of two cones rise like glaciers. *I woke up to the reality that I was screaming. Doris had to push through the bookshelf I had put in front of the door again. The patients had left at some point in the night. It was the first time that she had given them flowers.*

Melody opened the door for me with bright red lipstick on. She said she was having a party for her friends from school. We drank some whiskey together and went to the back room. People started to arrive. I grazed around in circles, popping in and out of different cycles of conversation, thinking back to the dream I had that was woven into Chapter Four. Melody's father's kitchen was tiled with white squares; the mortar was black. Beneath the cabinets, there was a fresco of a green man tumbling over himself again and again. Kids trickled out of the powder room, and I paced around the TV with the ones smoking joints and playing video games. "Kick in the Door" by Biggie Smalls was playing. Girls swayed in groups of three; boys huddled in circles. The white bodies moved in concentric shapes, avoiding the same word in all of their favorite songs. Then I was in Melody's room, smoking with others. Her friend Grace asked, "So how did you two meet?"

"I was going to visit my father's friend in the Hamptons . . ." And so for the first time I saw myself as part of her life. I had never considered what she had thought of me, if she had at all, in the time between August 2007, when we met at the carnival, and May 2009, when I brought the letter to her school. I had planned what she had seen as providence, yet had not considered what narrative she was writing about me, and did not want to. I excused myself from her room, found myself drinking in front of the mirror in the bathroom, and stayed for a while before returning to the party.

It was early. Then it was late. Melody kept staring at me from across the room, as if upset. I went to the bathroom for longer intervals of time, avoiding her closest friends. The classmates trickled out. I went to her room and we began to hold each other. She kissed me with a cloud of smoke in her mouth. The little white fan was on by the window. The room smelled like marijuana and tobacco when we lay down together.

"Did I embarrass you?"

"Embarrass?"

"With the story about how we met."

"No."

"Just no?"

"What else is there to say?" She shifted under the covers, turning to look at me. "Who are you?"

"What do you mean?" I said.

"Where were you born?"

"St. Luke's Roosevelt, four blocks from here."

"Parents? We have to talk through this at some point."

I inched closer, and she rubbed my chin off her shoulder. "I've never met my father. It doesn't make me angry or anything . . ."

"What does your mom say about him?"

"Not much."

"What does she look like?"

"She's black."

"I figured that, but what is her face like?"

"Pointy, doughy in the cheeks. Her eyes are brown."

"Does she have freckles like me?"

I kissed her near the nose, attempting to calm my nerves. "I guess she does."

We kissed each other on the mouth, and I tried to slide my tongue between her lips. She spat it out.

"What's her name?"

"Doris."

"What's she like?"

"I don't know."

"Nothing else?"

"She is an addict."

"So is Rick."

I tried to sound more convincing. "You don't understand. Sometimes I don't see her for days at a time."

"What does the doctor say?"

"I would prefer not to talk about it."

"Oh." Melody was silent for a while. "You aren't at health risk or anything?" I pointed at myself, and pretended to be offended by her insinuation. "I'm sorry." She picked up my right shoulder, nuzzled into my neck, and kissed the place where my throat met my collarbone; I descended to her chest.

"Stop."

"Why?" She opened her eyes. "Are my questions turning you on?"

"It's just spontaneity," I said and then inched closer; she pulled away. Though I was compelled to tell her the truth, Melody seemed to enjoy my anonymity, and even now, as she questioned me, she may have hoped for my life to remain a mystery. Though I had executed my plan to gain Melody's trust, I had not seen a future with her—I still could not see one. She inched closer.

"Will you meet my father?"

"Maybe."

"You don't want to meet him?"

"If you want me to, I will."

"He gets back in two weeks." She opened her mouth and then closed it, looked down at her hands.

OCTOBER 11, 2009

I was staring up at the neo-Gothic cathedral on St. Nicholas Terrace where my mother said she attended college in 1980 and 1989. I descended across St. Nicholas Park at 135th Street, weaving through the people coming from the mouth of the subway. I walked up Edgecombe Avenue to 137th Street and turned east, where I crossed two men walking south on Frederick Douglass, and continued toward Adam Clayton Powell Jr. Boulevard. I looked to my right and studied the apartment buildings with tiled walkways, brownstones with Romanesque windows. I looked at the façades, which were built neither like the old brownstones nor the new apartment buildings. Across the street, the houses were nearly identical, but the bricks ranged in color from maroon to orange instead of tan. They extended down the entire avenue, on both sides, in the same fashion. I approached a gate just like the others, with spiraling metalwork, and thought the designs were adinkra symbols, whose cultural origin was Akan.

The pattern had appeared on a gate my mother bought for the front door last spring. I realized that some further connection existed between the Akan culture, the gates, and the Europeans—easy to decipher, but of which I was ignorant. I carried these thoughts down Malcolm X Boulevard, toward the 2/3 station at 135th Street, where my eyes were arrested by a mural on the west side of Harlem Hospital. It was a triptych—three panels showed three different scenes. The northernmost was filled with the image of a black male conductor in a white suit, wand in hand, with a black man dancing in the background. In the second panel, a black male professor, black male student, black female doctor, and black female typist were captured mid-assignment. The third and last—a black farmer, his wife, and their child look out upon the city and a hot-air balloon. I had seen the art project in *Harlem: Two Centuries of Architecture*. It was followed by an account of New York's white citizens rallying around the removal of the mural in 1936. They believed "future generations" would not want to see this image on the front of their hospital. I thought to enter but did not. To view artwork in a hospital was too close a reminder that art is created out of others' misfortune. I paused in the street again, this time looking back at the steps I had taken—north, east, south—finding logic in my winding procrastination. I did not want to go to class yet. I grinned, though I was not certain why, which made me grin even wider, before I determined that these ritual trips to Harlem I made were not just to evade Melody's detection, but were also some sad attempt to redeem my mother. Everything I saw reminded me of her in some way that could have been sentimental if not for the state of our relationship. I was not in Harlem, I thought, but between Harlem and a place I had created through my mother's memory, also named Harlem. As I walked up the block, I could see my face in the rearview mirror of a silver pickup truck. I stopped there for a moment and looked at the way my lips spread, and suffered the impression that I was no longer clean. Not a slight uncleanliness that could be washed off in the shower. I tried to get to the bottom of this feeling, but my head began to vibrate, causing me to pause at the side of the road and sit back on my heels. There was a four-story brownstone in front of me that had a crescent-shaped balcony on the second floor.

The sun had just passed behind a cloud, and as I looked to the ground the weight of this building pushed down on me. I blinked, then looked back up to see a branch of the New York Public Library named after the Harlem Renaissance poet Countee Cullen, where the mansion had just been. It was far more ugly than what had stood in front of me before, which, I now realized, had been a figment of my imagination.

Inside the atrium were two statues of Countee Cullen attached by the same white wooden base. One was bronze and cut off at the waist. It was caressing the cheek of a white bust of Cullen, whose head was adorned with a wreath. I stood behind the bust and read:

ONLY THE POLISHED
SKELETON, OF FLESH RELIEVED
AND PAUPERIZED, CAN REST AT
EASE AND THINK UPON THE
WORTH OF ALL IT SO DESPISED.

I walked to the front desk, not sure where to start, or for what I was searching. "Do you have any books on Countee Cullen and Jean Toomer?"

"You might want to try next door."

"Sorry?"

"The Schomburg Center next door. They have a lot more books."

"Would you mind just checking for me?"

She stared over her glasses before typing the information into the keyboard. "It says there is a book of letters by Toomer that references Cullen."

"May I see the letters?"

"You may."

After the librarian directed me to the book, I thanked her and sat in the corner at a table for four.

The letters were not organized by recipient, but by the year in which they were written. I skimmed for names I knew, reading a letter from Toomer addressed to Alain Locke: "Of the two questions raised; why are universities sterile? And why are undergraduates stones." I learned, "Countee Cullen bought the first copy of *Cane* on sale . . . W. E. B. Du Bois liked it despite its modernist prose . . . Toomer began turning down requests for his work to be included in Negro anthologies," which was not something I had read about him before. I turned the page, to a letter Toomer wrote to his white mentor Waldo Frank. "A few generations from now, the negro will still be dark, and a portion of his psychology will spring from this fact, but in all else he will be a conformist to the general outlines of American civilization, or of American chaos. In my own stuff, in those pieces that come nearest to the old Negro . . . the dominant emotion is a sadness derived from a sense of fading, from a knowledge of my futility to check solution."

I went back to the introduction and read that Toomer had not even lived in Harlem during the Renaissance; he had stayed in Greenwich Village, on East Thirteenth Street. I put down the book, which was beginning to disgust me, and headed to the public computer, then typed "Jean Toomer" into the browser and skimmed over the images I recognized, until I saw a picture of him from the 1950s. Nathan "Jean" Pinchback Toomer was hunched over a pile of papers on his desk, wearing a dark jean jacket and staring down at the pages of a manuscript, like a man who had lost his mind by focusing too closely on the work. I felt heat coming from beneath my skin. I looked up from the

computer, scanning to the right, and the bronze torso of Countee Cullen stared at me from behind his white clay bust.

YET DO I
MARVEL AT THIS CURIOUS
THING: TO MAKE A
POET BLACK, AND BID
HIM SING

I returned to the front desk and requested a biography of
Jean Toomer.

As the '20s roared on, he became a disciple of the Russian
mystic George Gurdjieff, and by the '40s he was a Quaker. It
wasn't that he had wanted to become white. Toomer could trace
his origin to nine different ethnicities. Any stress placed on one
of his racial distinctions was false. Something was still bothering
me, and in my thoughts about Jean Toomer an unnerving question popped into my head. Was my desire for Melody caused by
a desire to be whiter? As I turned that thought over in my mind,
a body crashed into the chairs on my right side. Two men, both
over the age of forty, were wrestling. I stood up. The security
guard came to separate them, and now they were on either side
of me. The smaller one looked in my direction and said, "I better
never see you in Harlem again. You better never come back to
Harlem, motherfucker."

Through the tension, the firmly worded threat, I believed the
man was gesturing at me. It was a message from the God of Abra-
ham, and his voice was just the vessel. I left the library walking
west and felt myself between life and death, black and white,
home and Melody's apartment—all massive or minuscule in tangible or intellectual difference.

On the bus ride to Manhattan to meet Melody's father for the first time, I had decided to pick back through *Cane*. After an hour of reading, I began to feel wrathful. It happened in the chapter entitled "Seventh Street," where Jean Toomer wrote, "God would not dare to suck black red blood. A nigger God! He would duck his head in shame and call for the Judgment Day." I was conjuring this same God to do my bidding. Melody had asked me to come over on Saturday, then changed it to Friday, so I faked an illness at school, beginning the act at 10:00 a.m. I was dismissed by noon, which left me enough time to walk over to the bus stop and get to the city by 3:30—one hour before I was supposed to meet Melody and Rick. The journey had left me tired, though not physically, so I walked west to Madison Avenue, passing luxury stores, to Fifty-ninth Street, turning west again to the sound of horse-drawn carriages and the smell of shit, to the south of Central Park.

Melody's father had his green-framed sunglasses on, covering his eyes, which had been sensitive all afternoon, or so he said. We sauntered west at an uneven pace, Melody and me slightly behind him. On the corner of Sixty-first Street and Amsterdam, next to the Fordham Law School campus, a homeless man sat in a wheelchair. "How are you doing, brother!" he yelled.

"Maintaining, sir." The artist listened to the man, who wore a Vietnam War Veteran hat, and had a cart full of boxes and garbage bags. I nodded at him. He met my eyes, then glanced away. Rick dropped a ten-dollar bill into his cup. Melody nudged me.

"Classic capitalist guilt exchange," she whispered. Her father waited for two avenues to pass before he addressed her.

"What's that?"

"Of course he recognizes you, Dad. You give him ten dollars every time."

"So it means less? How many people listen to him on the street?"

"How many pay him?" They continued in this manner as we crossed into Central Park, where tourists drank overpriced coffee in expendable cups. The leaves were beginning to change, and a blond man was taking a picture of his wife in the middle of the bridge we were standing on. It overlooked the ice rink, which had yet to open this season. "We went to the Metropolitan Museum of Art together," I heard Melody say to Rick.

"Oh, God."

"I know." I looked for faces in the rock formations on the other side of the overpass, then down on the ice rink and back up at the skyscrapers on Fifty-ninth Street and Central Park South before I began to see a bull take shape in the rocks across from us, its tail adrift, its horns pressed forward. It seemed like a sign for my desire to write, but I was not sure what led me to make that association. I returned to the conversation that Melody and her father were having—"Heliopolitan Obelisk. Which has nothing to do with Cleopatra"—but I had no desire to join in. I looked back to the rocks as the bull had stretched to its limit— disappearing in the time that it took Melody to tap me on the shoulder, saying, "You want to eat?"

While we walked out of the park I imagined running in the opposite direction. I tried to keep calm, telling myself, "These urges are very human," but Rick and Melody continued to talk to each other, pronouncing all of their words correctly, and their sarcasm became cynical—I could not stop thinking I did not like either her or her father. After we finished eating, I stayed over. Richard locked the door to his room. "He said you could stay." And I smiled, because I did not have to get back on the train to Long Island tonight and cut writing class tomorrow. Melody brought me back to her room. In the moonlight, I was confronted with her glowing whiteness.

In the darkness, the only thing vivid is the outline of her birds. I feel my body jerking toward the hallway. My eyelids flutter. The tendon on the sole of my foot is in a ball. I lurch forward. The two doors in front of me are painted white and curved like a bell. There is an orange light coming from beneath the entrance. I appear inside a white padded room on a chair. There are hands on the back of my head. They are feeling my face now, trying to force my eyelids open. I woke up beside Melody with a scratch at the back of my throat. I stumbled around the bedroom, without light, and walked to the kitchen. The legs of a chair moved across the floor. Rick was sitting up and looking at the clock. It was 2:21 a.m. As I entered, he did not acknowledge my presence, which made my sleeping with his daughter feel irresponsible. I went to fill a glass of water from the wood-paneled refrigerator, then he said, "My father grew up in this neighborhood. It didn't look like this in the forties and fifties." The glass was full. As I made my way back to the door, he interrupted—"It was called San Juan Hill before. Like the battle in Cuba. A lot of blacks, a lot of Hispanics, you know, from Hispaniola." He went silent again.

"It's a palimpsest," I said. He did not respond, so I continued, "The Amsterdam Houses, you know, you living here—some of the stuff of the old community remains."

"You are smart." I could see he liked that I had connected him with the neighborhood—though he probably did not want to live in a community with its former residents.

"Thank you, Mr. Gilbert."

"Just call me Rick."

"OK." I watched his facial expression change back to pensive while he continued to stare at the clock: 2:24. I pushed back through the hallway and lay down beside Melody again. From her window, looking east, you could see the little tower that resembled the top of a lit cigarette. I reached the side of her bed, propped her window open, and smoked—like I had seen her do. She rustled in her dream, never quite waking, uttering one word—"timing."

OCTOBER 24, 2009

When I woke up next to Melody at 10:33, Rick was not home. We dressed quickly and walked up Central Park West, past the Trump International Tower at Sixtieth Street, to the entrance of the park. Melody directed me down the footpath, through a tunnel where she yelled "Hello!" just to hear her voice echo. We sat on the boulders south of the baseball fields and a patch of sand. It was 58 degrees outside. I read that on the digital box atop 1740 Broadway, right beneath the southern end of Central Park; it flashed the weather and time, one after the other, in five-second intervals. She was rolling a joint. Her fingers curled around the bleached piece of paper, and I wondered how many times she had done this before.

"Are you nervous?" she asked.

"No."

"The cops don't come up here." She continued at her task, not stopping to look up or breathe, until she was licking the gum on the side of the paper, making the plant mixture into a cone.

"Does Rick talk to you about his father?"

"Oh God. Did he tell you about the gambling?"

"No. He said his father used to live in this neighborhood."

"I don't listen to him when he talks about his dad."

"Why not?"

"His dad was a fake."

"A fake?"

"His father was a complete phony."

"How was he phony?"

"You can't tell him I told you."

"You know I'm not going to tell."

"You can't tell anybody."

"What is it?"

"His father passed."

"What do you mean passed?"

"He was black, and after college, he was white. He grew up here, went to school, stopped seeing his parents, then married my grandmother as Richard Murzynowics." She chuckled while exhaling a cloud of smoke from the joint. "Rick tried to find his family, but his dad wouldn't let him, so they had a falling-out. It's the reason his art was any good."

Her eyelids were low from the marijuana; when she turned to face me, the sense that she was involving me in some great deception became palpable. I did not let her know these thoughts, though. I lay on her stomach, and we stared up at the clouds for a while.

"I have to go."

"Why don't you come over tomorrow?"

"I have to help my mother with something."

"Just come over at night before I go to sleep."

"I wish I could." She frowned, tried to light the joint again.

On the train ride to class, a homeless man pushed an elderly concertgoing couple out of the way. His socks had been ripped to tan shreds; pus came from the side of one shoe, ankles puffy, legs bent like each step was sending a knife through his shins.

"Stand clear of the closing doors, please."

His gray locks were interspersed with white tufts. As he passed, I noticed the back of his head was a dark brown—the hair sat against it like a halo. "Change! Change!" He stopped in front of a twenty-something Caucasian man—"Change! Change!" The glasses dipped down the man's nose as he fumbled in the leather wallet for money—"Change!" He parted with five dollars—"Change!" He found twenty-five more cents and the older man continued to the next car. He opened the door. Noise from the tunnel blew through the cabin; he extended his right arm. The door closed behind him. The image stuck in my mind. His posture—the way he raised his arm, it was like the bronze statue of Countee Cullen caressing his own cheek. I was developing a madness, one in which American fiction was becoming part of my life.

Act

III

Chapter 5

My grandmother's favorite saying was tacked to a placard above the garbage can in the kitchen. "You are too blessed to be stressed." To its right hung my aunt's, "Sometimes I get so tired then I think of what Harriet Tubman had to do." That was Doris. She was overweight with ashen teeth and two hues darker than my mother. In the living room, beneath the picture of my great-grandfather with a pipe in his mouth, Doris kept a bowl of cigarettes. The summer breeze pushed through the screen door, which was ripped in places. I took the fly swatter to the back porch and killed eight bees. She came out with a book in her hand entitled Treat It Gentle. *Its cover photo was black and white and featured a man grasping a soprano saxophone, his arms raised and bent at the elbows. When my aunt saw the bees' small lifeless bodies on the porch, she hit me with the book. I cried. She never hit me again.*

I loved the way Doris told stories more than anything else. Showing me pictures in a photo album, she began: "This was my grandmother, the one from Virginia," or "my father, the Mason." Her mother was an angel, supposedly, and by asking no questions, I left my grandmother's memory as such. "Your grandfather had been a door-to-door salesman for most of his life in Hoboken. Then he worked construction for black families on Long Island. That is how he bought the land this house was built on, and that little plot for the church. He told me he was a child preacher somewhere in Virginia. I think he started after the church was completed, but I am not sure. The Wesleys were always good storytellers. You could never tell their facts from their fictions."

"Can we see the church?" She inhaled her cigarette by the screen door in the living room.

"Some rich white man bought it, tore it down, and built a corny house on the land."

"Why is it corny?"

"Because it looks like every other rich white person's house, in any beach town on Long Island." She went on to explain the difference between the black aesthetic and the white aesthetic, always beginning after emancipation. She said, "The difference is the way we see the world. Their Lost Generation was our Renaissance." Then she would go on about Langston Hughes or Zora Neale Hurston, switching to Louis Armstrong or Bessie Smith. All the historical figures, our black cultural superheroes, fought a decisive battle to redefine American culture, but they had lost, or so it appeared to Doris. "That cultural loss can be sensed in everything," she said, "from the music we listen to, to the way our houses are built." One time I pointed at a house; "White," she said. A black man walked out. She said, "Still white."

"How can a black person's house be white?"

"The people do not determine the color of the house; the architect does. Take Osgood Mason or Van Vechten, for example . . ." Even a discussion about this town's architecture could lead her to refer to some white figure from the 1920s who aided in the death or creation of the Harlem Renaissance. She never told these stories about race when a couple was visiting for a healing. Often they were rich. I could tell by their cars. Often they were distraught, and Doris read these couples by the things they carried, the things they said, and the things they felt but would not express. Her philosophy could be learned, but at a cost. It was all in the books she'd read.

"All books," she said, "do two things. They open and close certain valves of understanding. If you read a math book, you learn that one plus one equals two. You get the system of numbers, thus opening your mind to a new world of understanding. Nevertheless, it does something else. Every time you see the markings, one plus one equals two, you recognize it within the context of a mathematical system. The numbers no longer have infinite meanings—just the ones humans have assigned them. Now you are closed off to the world of questions about numbers, like: What does it mean if I say one is not a whole number?"

The fact that Doris lived two minutes from a beach yet never stepped foot in the water was an example she used to prove her existential point: "I know what I should fear in the water, and I can't unknow it. Although, to know is not important, nor is not to know, but to be comfortable in your ignorance is." She spoke to me like an adult, and there was not a question she would answer untruthfully, except the ones involving my mother.

OCTOBER 30, 2009

I was becoming upset with the propensity my fiction had of seeming as if a white man had written it, and as I composed Chapter Five I recognized that all the episodes in my incomplete novel suffered from the same type of inauthenticity. Everything Doris did conformed to some stereotype that I had not meant to convey when I first sat down to write the story. She was too strange, too wise—a favorable rewriting of my mother. I couldn't rid myself of the feeling that the sentences were a product of something inside me that was appropriating blackness. I knew it to be true, and I could not divorce this revelation from my research into Jean Toomer's identity. The train doors shut at Thirty-fourth Street. I had gotten off at Penn Station, ridden up to 125th Street on the A train, as I was used to doing, then boarded the downtown D, which I did not usually do, so I missed the Fifty-ninth Street stop. The reason to continue seeing Melody no longer made sense to me. I was being carried forward by habit. I left my seat, bypassing three women who wore red face paint and pointed ears, to view the subway map at the other end of the car. I followed the orange D line until it reconnected with the A, C, and B at West Fourth Street. I noticed the small green patch above that bordered the words "Washington Square Park." The train pulled forward, and I was driven off balance. I stumbled back, noticing that the map resembled two lovers embracing: she is above him. Her eyes are Pelham Bay Park, in the Bronx. His lips are parted in Brooklyn, at Newtown Creek. We stopped moving. Through

92

the window, I saw "Baal" written against the black subway wall.

I exited the station at West Eighth Street, heading north, and stood on a traffic island, watching small plane lights appear in the darkness behind One World Trade Center. I heard pieces of conversation: "Tonight?" "That's crazy." "Memphis." The sounds were layered atop car horns and an ambulance in the distance. At the corner of West Tenth Street and Avenue of the Americas, there was a maroon castle. It had spires and stained-glass windows—I mistook it for a church. The gate was black, and between the iron bars I saw the same Akan symbol as in Harlem. I continued east on West Tenth, stopping at four different gates on the north side of the block to look at the adinkra that continued to appear. On Fifth Avenue, doormen replaced the iron bars; the low residential buildings became ten-story Art Deco edifices. I looked right and left until Washington Mews, seeing the arch in Washington Square Park. There were two sculptures of George Washington on either side. It imitated France's national monument, the Arc de Triomphe, which had been appropriated from the Roman Empire. Feelings of patriotism did not move me. My shadow appeared under the streetlamps as I approached them, disappearing as I moved on to the next. Near West Fourth Street, a security guard escorted two young men out of a bar named the Fat Black Pussycat. The smaller one put his leather coat on, smoothing the left sleeve, before saying, "Fuck this fucking place anyway." They continued east, and I went west to catch the A to Columbus Circle. Melody opened the door for me.

"You didn't want to go out on Halloween?"

"Halloween is for children." She was upset. "I'm surprised your mother let you come out." Rick was not there. We went to her room. She had been working with watercolor again and kept referring to the giant purple orbs on her canvases as "the universal." It was not well defined, but she wouldn't work with one concept for too long. I had heard nothing about photography since she had abandoned the instant camera in late September.

"The universal what?"

"Oneness as representation." I attributed her current state of aggression to the problems she was trying to solve in her work, which seemed topical now. "How come I never see you writing?"

I lay on her bed. "I'm not writing anymore." Every ten minutes she nudged my leg, alerting me to the passing time.

"This would all be different if we could see each other on the weekdays."

I rolled over, put the covers around my shoulders.

"Can I meet your mother?" The pitch of her voice gave the words a threatening tone.

OCTOBER 31, 2009

I woke up from a dream I could not remember and was upset with Melody. She was still asleep on her side. I got up and roamed into the living room. Everything was quiet. I turned on the light, then continued around the apartment, past the kitchen, toward Rick's bedroom. Something was calling me inside. I went into the closet with the jackets in different patterns and colors to see if he had hidden something there. I searched the room for some clue as to what I was looking for, when it became apparent that this blind search was some strange metaphor for my life. Instead of continuing, I went to the bookshelf next to his door and read some titles. There were books of poetry, art, and Zen, which made me chuckle. It was a less imposing collection than Doris's. It felt wrong to open the books, so I ran my fingers over all the spines before going back to Melody's room. She was coming out of the bathroom. "You are a chronic sleepwalker."

"I know."

She kissed me. "I'm going on some fancy school trip to Québec for two and a half weeks."

"When?"

"Friday." She put her right hand under my shirt, "Can I meet your mother when I get back?" Then she pushed me onto the bed.

"This is a strange time to ask me that."

"I know, but I just thought of it."

"Maybe."

"I'm fine with maybe."

She unzipped my pants, taking my penis, no stiffer than a bag of water, holding the head inside her mouth, maintaining eye contact with me, and for the first time I began to feel something like remorse for the lie I had been telling. "I don't think it's going to get hard right now."

"What's wrong?" It was softened by my desire to continue lying.

"Nothing." My eyes began to water.

"This hasn't happened before."

"I know that."

"You can tell me anything. You understand that, right?"

"I know that." I could feel her reaching out to hug me, but I went to the closet where my clothes lay in a pile and began to dress.

"Are you going to say something?"

"I'll see you before you leave."

"Do you promise?"

"Yes." We kissed each other. She was licking and biting my lip, and I had the desire to push her, or yell, or show her how angry these small affections made me, but I closed my eyes, smiled once or twice, then walked to the A train.

I was standing on West Tenth Street looking at the building I had seen last weekend, with the Akan symbol in its gate. In the atrium, there was an exhibit, showing the different institutions that had existed on this corner beginning in 1833, when the land grounded a fire lookout tower. The architects Calvert Vaux and Frederick Clarke Withers billed the city $360,000 for the erection of a courthouse and market in the Victorian Gothic style in 1876. The Jefferson Market Courthouse reached its height of fame in 1906, when Harry K. Thaw was formally charged with the murder of the renowned architect Stanford White. By 1929, it had become a detention center for women. It wasn't until 1961, when the community activists Margot Gayle and Philip Wittenberg decided the lot would best be used as a public library and garden, that the building became what it was then, the Jefferson Market Library. I walked down the stairs to the reference room where the brick buttresses retained the slightest hint of its history as a gallows. Although not designed as a library, it was more suited to house books than the haphazard interior of the Countee Cullen. It made me want to go to school in a place with façades such as these, in a far-off place. I headed upstairs to the second floor, stopping to note the intricacy of the stained-glass windows, advancing into the main room while wondering about this Victorian Gothic style, how works of architecture were classified. I found a reference book from the early 2000s that covered the discipline's development from 4000 B.C.E. through 1990 C.E. First, I looked for "gates" in the index, but the subject did not have one corresponding section. I focused on the section labeled "American Neo-classicism," which began with a passage about Calvert Vaux, the man who had designed this building. He also designed Central Park with the help of Frederick Law Olmsted, which was then built on top of slave burial grounds and the city's first settlement of free blacks. First was the architect Henry Hobson Richardson, then his trusted disciple, Stanford White, the man who had appeared in the atrium's exhibit. I read on, believing the connections between the building and the book would lead me to an understanding about the sign that was in the gate.

White was the son of a Shakespearean scholar. At eighteen, he became principal assistant to Richardson, a post he would man for six years before traveling to Europe to study classical architecture. He returned to the United States and joined the firm of Charles Follen McKim and William Rutherford Meade. One of the major projects the firm designed was the old Madison Square Garden (1889, Italian Revival) on Twenty-sixth Street. It was yellow and white, and made of terra-cotta bricks. There were two separate auditoriums, a garden, and a nude statue of Diana, the Roman goddess of childbirth. It was said that Stanford White had fashioned an apartment beneath the observation tower. In the center of the living room, attached to the thirty-foot ceiling, was a velvet swing, which White would use, after a bout of coitus, to push his female partners so high that their faces could kiss the ceiling. One of these young women was the fourteen-year-old Evelyn Nesbit, who had worked as a live model for artists and photographers around the city. Her image became so ubiquitous that, although she had been born to a poor Pennsylvania family and taken advantage of in her youth, she catapulted to fame and notoriety, rising high enough in social standing to marry Harry Kendall Thaw, heir to a Coca-Cola and railroad fortune. On the night of June 25, 1906, Stanford White attended a play, *Mam'zelle Champagne*, with his son, in the Madison Square Garden he had designed seventeen years prior, just a staircase away from the velvet swing. Also in attendance were Thaw and his wife, Nesbit. As the chorus began to sing the popular song "I Could Love a Million Girls," Harry K. Thaw left his wife's side and walked within two feet of Stanford White. When the heir raised his pistol, onlookers heard him say, "You have ruined my wife." He pulled the trigger three times, separating the right half of White's face from his head. What caused Thaw to kill White is ultimately unknowable, though the court deemed he had suffered a temporary bout of insanity. The final sentence of this lengthy section read, "Stanford White's son hopes he is remembered for his masterpieces such as the Four Chimneys Estate in New Rochelle or the Arch in Washington Square Park."

I put down the book and wondered why such a large section was devoted to the smut trial of a minor American architect. I thought, all history books rely on the overinflated legacy of privileged men. After that, I tried to figure out if *Mam'zelle Champagne* was a minstrelized version of a play called *Mademoiselle Champagne*, but the search engine on the library's computer gave me no matching results. I put the book back in its place and walked to the A train at West Fourth Street, passing the gate outside again, knowing I had not found what I was searching for.

Rick came to the door. "How are you feeling, Davy Crockett?" He had called me last week. Melody was still away in Québec. He came across more somberly on the phone than in person. The two of us were supposed to meet at his house at 3:00. I knew I would not make it to the writer's workshop this week, again. "I thought we could go out to eat."

I shrugged. "Great."

We ascended Broadway, passed the Starbucks, and entered Lincoln Square Pavilion—an outdoor atrium for the City Ballet, Opera House, and Philharmonic.

"Thelonious Monk lived on San Juan Hill. The jazz guy. It was a family type of neighborhood. My father lived somewhere over there," he said, pointing to the Library of the Performing Arts. "Palimpsest, right?"

I looked around at the buildings—the concert venues, Juilliard, and a rusted sculpture, and did not feel this place was a palimpsest: the black history left no trace; Lincoln Square was a premeditated act of erasure. We continued around the pavilion, made a right on Sixty-fifth Street back to Broadway, passing the Century 21 on Sixty-sixth before stopping at a Japanese restaurant on Sixty-ninth, where he said he used to take Melody's mother. We sat in a booth by the window. I was wondering if Jean Toomer had ever visited Stanford White's Four Chimneys Estate. White's murder had occurred fewer than twelve months before Nina Pinchback had moved to New Rochelle with her new husband and teenage son, Jean.

"Wow. Deep in thought."

"Sorry."

"I can tell you are dealing with a lot." I had not been focusing on Rick because my head was still in the library, but as I came to, I could see he was withholding something from me.

"We are alike, you and me," Rick said.

"What is this about, Mr. Gilbert?"

"I want to tell you a story about my father. He was a serious man. He taught me all about Robert Moses and housing discrimination and how difficult it must have been for black Americans. Never once did he mention his mother or father. He would warn me—don't let your family demons become your own." Rick broke our gaze, trying to sense whether Melody had told me about his father or not. "This is not where I wanted to start."

"Start what?"

"Our conversation." He sighed and looked off. "Melody told me about your issues, and before you get upset—"

"What issues?"

"With your mother. You know, we've got off on the wrong foot here. I say we eat our food and talk when we are done eating." Then, after dinner, he said, "You're going to be so blown away by this surprise, I'm not going to ruin it. Let's put our headphones on so that I cannot ruin it." Before I could respond, the little red buds were in his ears. We boarded the A train, which moved past Fulton Street and continued into a tunnel, then Brooklyn, and got off at Hoyt-Schermerhorn, transferring to the G to Clinton-Washington. He was wearing his headphones the whole time. Rick walked up to a brownstone and descended the short flight of stairs to the lower apartment. He tapped on the brick next to the doorbell three times, to show me it was hollow, before pulling the block out and dropping the key into his hand.

The apartment was simple; the front door opened to a living room, followed by a bedroom and a kitchen. All of the walls were painted cream. There were boxes stacked next to a sofa near the entrance. Though no one seemed to live there, its bareness reminded me of Rick's. "Well? What do you think?"

"I think it's an apartment." He took off the headphones and grabbed me by the shoulders.

"I had some guys clean it up, and now—just think of it as a safe house. You don't have to *take* the key, but you know where it is. You get it." Like it was a joke, or something passing by the lens of a camera—did you catch it?

"Why are you doing this?"

"Because you need help."

"I didn't ask you for help."

"But those who need it the most often don't ask. Listen, listen, listen. I don't want to argue with you, I do that enough with my daughter. Do you want to stay here tonight?"

"No."

We left the basement entrance, and the red headphones hung around his white jacket. Rick stood out against the night. I watched him, the way his body swayed to catch his weight, the predetermined strut, practiced and meditated upon.

For the duration of our train ride—catching glimpses of him checking for my eyes in the window across from us—I felt as though Rick had been waiting for me to appear in his life. He stared at me not as a human, but as a symbol for a larger group of people who were suffering. It was offensive, yet still, I tapped his shoulder near Thirty-fourth Street; he removed his headphones, and I made sure to express my gratitude for the safe house. I stayed on the express train to 125th Street after he got off at Columbus Circle, walked up the stairs, then descended to the downtown platform.

NOVEMBER 15, 2009

An iPhone sat on the counter charging in the safe house. It had no password. I was sure Rick had left it for me, knowing I would not have accepted it if he had offered. I turned off the frying pan and put the eggs on a plate next to strips of bacon. The *Law & Order* television marathon would run until late in the afternoon. My notebook was sitting in the corner of the living room. The scenes I had written since I stopped going to the libraries in Harlem were stale. I had not been to class in two weeks and had lost control of the narrative. Though I could see how the story would end, I did not want to write the final scene because, when it was finished, I would be left to write the small, ugly details in the middle chapters. I wanted to put the energy wasted on fiction back into my life, so I thought of ways to make the safe house more my own. The Internet told me there was a flea market just four stops away, so I put on my coat, gloves, and hat, before heading to the subway at Clinton-Washington. I looked at the Fort Greene brownstones on my way to the train, distinct from those in West Harlem, and saw again the symbol that resembled a cursive heart in the design of the gates. I typed "adinkra," "Akan," "symbols" into the cellular phone, and clicked on the "Images" tab. There I found a page with aphorisms represented by symbols. I recognized the one I had seen as "sankofa," and the phone said the symbol originated in the Twi language. It meant to bring what is good from the past into the present. I looked up at St. James and

Atlantic and did not recognize the neighborhood, so I went to the phone's map application and found my way back to the train.

The flea market block was quiet. There was a coffee shop with a squeaky door, a children's apparel store, and a soul food restaurant. Some young men roamed in groups of three or four—women pushed shopping carts, and white men tried hard not to look into my eyes. I didn't like standing long at lights, because the block made me feel uneasy. This uneasiness made me think of Melody, so I tried to remember what I had liked about her after our first date to calm my mind. I began repeating, "curiosity, openness, honesty," things I did respect, in a way, but did not entirely practice. I looked to my right. The flea market seemed to be closed. A man came out and pulled on the gate, a brown newsboy cap sitting low on his head. I crossed the street so as to avoid the men in the neighborhood, and noticed two cops standing on the corner, so I stopped, crossed back, and raised the police's suspicions. I tried not to turn to face them, but I did, twice. They were walking in my direction. I gathered speed, passing the train station at Utica that I had exited; they did as well. We crossed St. Johns Park then Park Place before they were right beside me, and as my breath became short they passed me by without saying a word. I was not sure how far I had walked. The street names—Malcolm X then Park Place— were the same as in Manhattan. I pulled up the map on my phone again, and found myself on Eastern Parkway, looking up to see a man selling incense, and a line of young oak trees. I sent Melody a message—

Me: I miss you. 4:12 p.m.

It was not true. Her impending return cast a spell over me: doom. I looked up from the phone to see the green banisters of the 2 train. I transferred to the 1 train at Chambers Street, and took it to Houston. I arrived at the writers' workshop without the ten thousand words Jim had asked us to prepare for class.

Melody: I miss you too. 5:16 p.m.

Melody asked me over when she got back from her trip. It lasted three days longer than she had expected. I wanted to talk to her about the safe house, but somehow I knew she knew, and she knew I knew, we were not supposed to talk about it. Melody had put sheets on the floor in the living room, and put whiskey and popcorn on top of the sheets. It was an indoor picnic, she said. I began to drink.

"So what's it like in Harlem?" she asked. I spoke about St. Nicholas and the Countee Cullen library but avoided mentioning Jean Toomer, afraid I would become too passionate about his decision not to identify as a Negro, and offend her. It seemed as if Melody was expecting me to say more. "Do you have friends?" I told her that Meat lived in the building, and as I was conceiving more lies, the doorbell rang. I jumped. I ate too much food. She wanted to talk and drink more. We took our clothes off dutifully and lay in bed. I was overcome with the feeling that we should not know each other at all.

I woke upset. It was drizzling. Melody wanted to take a walk, so she gave me one of Rick's raincoats and we left the apartment. There wasn't much talking. Outside, Christopher Columbus was hunched over atop his statue on Fifty-ninth Street. To his right was a monument built for the battleship *Maine*, an American boat that blew up in the harbor of Havana in 1898. The statue featured Columbia, American goddess of liberty. I remembered the last two lines of a Phyllis Wheatley poem that my mother had made me memorize as a child. "Fix'd are the eyes of nations on the scales / for in their hopes Columbia's arm prevails." The statue seemed to have nothing to do with the battleship it was commemorating. We walked north and stopped at a small brown bench near Seventy-ninth Street to share a cigarette. I saw Melody in pieces. Her expensive jacket, her brooding silence, her hungover eyes, the way she inhaled the smoke all seemed ridiculous, so I looked away. Tourists crowded around hot dog carts next to the Museum of Natural History just two blocks north. Human life felt alien to me.

"This is certainly the end," I thought to myself, though I did not want it to be. I held Melody's hand tight, as if that could bring us closer. Our green and yellow raincoats stood out against the stone wall Vaux and Olmsted had designed to encircle Central Park. I looked back and could see what this island had been before—trees and hills. The entrance to Seneca Village had been six blocks farther north. It had been named after a Native American tribe or a Roman poet or a corruption of "Senegal." No landmark exists; now it is an area for recreation.

The rain began to pick up. Melody grabbed my hand and we walked to the front of the museum, where she pointed at a statue. Theodore Roosevelt sat on an unnamed horse, next to an unnamed black man in shackles and an unnamed Native American in tribal dress. They were cast in solid bronze, facing the park. She could see that I didn't like the statue, and of course she didn't like it either, but she seemed to like staring at it, in a way I found base.

"At least it tells the truth," she said. I felt hate for her and the instincts she gave words to, as if these words were profound. "What are you thinking about?" Although his father's passing for white had left Rick emotionally crippled, it seemed on the surface to have had no lasting effect on Melody.

"Do you know anything about Native American history, slavery?"

"I have learned about slavery, David."

"I'm not asking if you were assigned Howard Zinn; I'm asking if you feel part of it."

"That is what you were thinking about?"

"I just want to know why you find this statue entertaining."

"I don't find it entertaining. It's just here." Her words diminishing history, human suffering. "Why are you looking at me like that?" I thought about who I was, who I was becoming. "At least they aren't buried."

"Have you ever tried to say the word *nigger* before?"

She frowned at me. "Why are you so angry?"

"Say it."

She pulled the hood of her coat back on and went downtown.

Me: I'm sorry. It's an ugly statue. 8:05 p.m.

Melody: Come get drunk, stupid. 8:22 p.m.

Melody and I finished the fifth of whiskey Rick had stored in the freezer. She left *Law & Order* on the TV in her living room, and as we continued past our fifth shots, we pretended to be officers Tutuola and Benson. I watched her breasts bounce, milk white in the wintertime, carefree and childish, in a way that made me uncomfortable. She stopped playacting and said, "I knew you would behave differently. I should have never told you about my grandfather."

"I am the same as always." Her frown turned into a smile, and what I had seen in her before, awareness and intelligence, had been her self-conscious prodding, searching for approval from me that she did not find in herself. She whispered: "Can I show you something?" I nodded my head. She grabbed my forearm and pulled me into Rick's bedroom. It was a mess of clothing, and the TV hadn't been turned off after he left. A desk and easel were set up in the corner, like in her room, though his easel was covered in paint and his desk had small ideas collected on it in figures made of copper wire and nails. She excused her father's room. "It's messy, I know." We stopped by the bedside table, and for a moment I was sure she would pull out some drug that she had found, but at the bottom of this red drawer there was a black box. "You can't judge me. It's just . . . well, Rick showed it to me, and I feel like there is this dirty secret I have to share with someone."

The picture inside was a college scene; there was a frat house with Ionic columns, the number 282 above the doorway. It was sunny out, and there were seven white men crowded around a trophy. Two of them were holding it up. The other five, posed in various ways, slightly behind the first two, were arranged in a semicircle. You could just make out the date, 1954, on the bottom of the trophy.

"My grandfather is second on the left. The best man at his wedding is holding the trophy on the right side. I have never shown anyone this. I'm sure you can guess why." Richard Sr. was looking at the camera; he was wearing a red cap and a football jersey. Although he was not scowling, compared with the jovial nature of the rest of the scene he appeared to be upset. The two men in the middle, both in long white stockings with bow ties on, had used burnt cork to coat their faces black. "It was a ceremony that happened every year. It was called the Kake Walk. Thousands of people came from all over Vermont for one weekend, just to see this. They had skits, and singing, and parades. It was like prom but it was in February. He was a runner-up for the Kake Walk King that year. A good-looking man in a horrible kind of way."

Melody looked into my eyes for a reaction. I forced myself to grin, which she liked, puckering her lips as she backed away from me to the mass of clothes on Rick's bed. Her legs opened a fraction. I still had the photograph in my hand. I placed it back in the box, being gentle, and got into the bed. I lay behind her and put my penis between her legs, staring at the mullions in the window with my eyes squinted so that I could just make out a cross at the center. The light from the TV reflected on the side of her face in blue flashes that lasted four or five seconds at a time. Her feet were in my hands. I lifted my head and came inside her without wearing a condom. We lay naked after we had finished.

I wake up. All of the furniture in my room is next to the bed. The bookshelf, desk, and dresser are all draped in Melody's clothes. Everything is covered in orange goo. I wipe the crust from my eyes and begin to walk down the hallway toward the bathroom. The walls are light blue. A door opens. I enter. On the sink, outlined in seashells, there lies a toothbrush, a comb, and a tin of shoeshine. In the mirror, I see the back of the bathroom door. A red cape hangs with the words "Mister Interlocutor" on it. I wash the shoeshine into the sink, picking up the cloak. There is a calendar on the wall where it had hung. Melody had left me in her father's room. I covered myself and walked along the hallway to her room. As I stood in the doorway and watched her rest peacefully, I understood again that this life I was living with her was wrong. I walked to the backpack, removed the notebook, slipped into the bathroom, and began to write over the sink.

NOVEMBER 22, 2009

I jumped from my sleep. Melody was smoking a cigarette out the window. It was 11:00 a.m. I could not separate my dream from the events that had transpired the previous night. To give the occurrences more definition in my mind, I picked up the phone by my pants and searched for "Kake Walk Vermont." I then watched a video of two young white men in blackface parading around a gym. I typed in "Harlem Renaissance, blackface, Kake Walk."

"When am I going to meet your mother?" She had put the cigarette out and was standing in the bathroom. Her nipples were raised because she turned off the heat at night before she went to sleep. The question seemed to come from nowhere, but as I looked into the mirror at her back, I could see my notebook sitting on the sink next to the toothpaste.

"I didn't say you could read that."

"When am I going to meet your mother?"

"You can't."

"What do you mean I can't?"

"I mean you can't."

"Where does she live?"

"Harlem."

"Where?"

"At 362 West 127th Street."

"Does she know about me?"

"In her own way."

"What does that mean?"

"It means she wouldn't approve of our relationship. I don't like to talk about it." I spoke precisely in order to move past the conversation. "Do you speak Spanish?"

"Why are you changing the subject?"

"What subject?"

"Your mother. She doesn't know about me?"

"This is what you want to pick a fight about?"

"I'm not picking a fight. I just want to know why I can't meet your mother."

"I'm sure you will eventually."

"Why not now?"

"Right now?"

"Right now."

"She is relapsing again."

Melody's expression changed.

I went to the bathroom door and saw myself in the mirror. My jaw was clenched and my fists were balled. I unfurled them and went to hug Melody.

"I know it's hard to understand."

"I'm sorry."

"It's all right." I rested my chin on her shoulder and tightened my right arm before grabbing the notebook with my left and slipping it behind my back.

Final Chapter

You walked to the gate and pressed the bell next to the red door of the safe house before knocking. Nothing. You grabbed the brick and looked for the key, but it was not there. You banged on the door again. A rumbling. I saw your eyes through the curtains in the front window. "I figured you would just show up at some point." You kept your hair in a bun. It made you look narrow. I opened the door.

There were papers all over the living room, and a sandwich from last week sat on the chair beneath the desk. I invited you into the kitchen for a pot of tea. We sat at the teal table with wicker chairs, just below a poster of your father's work The City's Forgotten, *which I had bought from the visitors' center in the Metropolitan Museum of Art. Next to this poster was a group of stick figures that resembled crows. Each of them was scratched into the wall with a knife. You shifted in your seat. Just* beneath your shorts, I could see the black marks of a tattoo. I wrote something on the piece of paper in front of me.

"What are you doing?"

"I've been writing as the mood hits me." You turned your head sideways, but said nothing else, so I started to write again, pressing the pen harder into the sheet of paper.

"My father doesn't want you in here anymore."

"OK." It was not how I thought our first conversation after so many months apart would go. You stood up from the table and went to the refrigerator for water. There were crumbs and three sets of silverware (spoon knife, spoon knife, fork knife) on the table next to keys on a copper ring. The ring was attached to a pendant in the shape of the old World Trade Center.

"Rick told me you were living here, but how could I believe that?"

"I haven't been living here the whole time."

"Stop lying, David."

"I'm being serious."

"It's like you were fucking me for this apartment." You came back to the table and sat down. I saw the yellow in your gray irises, wrote it down, and as I diverted my attention you slapped the table, raised your fingers to my face. "He spoke to your mother, did you know that? Doris Wesley." You cut your head sideways and looked at me with those demeaning eyes.

"I'm sorry."

"I want you to seek help. I don't want you in my life in any way."

"Just stop and think."

"I don't need to—"

"Forgive me and I can leave—"

"You will leave either way."

"Just shut your mouth. Stop talking and forgive."

You backed up. "You still just don't get it. The thought of you coming near me, the thought of us laughing togethe—"
KNIFE WAS DRIVEN DOWN, fracturing and splintering the wood, down and down and down, into the table in the same place. Beige, brown, and copper flakes flew in patterns. You shook, and shadows came into the house from the backyard.

"Out."

"I have things here."

"Out!"

I grabbed my jacket from the chair, sending it crashing to the floor, and slid the notebook from the table before leaving. The moon was waning. I reached into my pocket to grab a cigarette. A gray oak was just behind me. I heard someone whisper your name. I looked down and regained composure.

After the last student had left the classroom, I approached Jim's desk. "I enjoyed the switch to the second person," he said.

"Thank you."

He shifted his weight to the desk. "I did expect you to have more, though, with all of the classes you missed, but I guess I can't give you an F now, can I?"

"Sorry."

"It's fine, David. I think you have to develop the relationship between the protagonist and Melody now." I nodded. "There is something in your writing. We just have to bring it out." Jim clenched his fists and turned them inward, to indicate grabbing hold of the narrative. "If you can take another tier-three class, then I'll see if we can't get you into tier four at half price, for the summer semester."

At the station, I stared at the mosaic of dolphins until they appeared to be a random assortment of cones and circles. I got on the train. There weren't many people there. My head rested against the wall of the car.

"Chambers Street."

I jumped off as the train doors closed because I had been traveling in the wrong direction. People in transit brushed by me as I sat on the platform floor. I felt like the station was closing in on me, so I exited and began to walk along Warren Street, hoping that the fresh air would soothe me. I turned in to City Hall Park. Halfway down the path I turned left, making out Horace

Greeley's name on the statue next to Tweed Courthouse. I pulled the phone out of my pocket to type their names in, and saw this message from Melody.

Melody: What are you doing for Christmas? 7:23 p.m.

As I clicked on the Internet application, the phone ran out of battery. I was not sure where to go. I turned left at Centre Street, looking right to the Manhattan borough president's office. I could only see the three brightest stars in Orion's belt. All the buildings were colonial white; the streets were empty. It reminded me of some dream I had on a night long ago. I could not remember when it had occurred. Chambers Street, then Reade Street; I kept going north until there was a fork in the road. Figuring it would be smarter to go in the direction I was familiar with, toward the west side, I followed Centre Street up to Foley Square, and was not paying attention to the direction I had come from when I found myself in the shadows of hopelessness. The desire to write fiction had led me here. I tried to remember if it was rooted in something good from my past. *Reach back and get it.* Still, I could not discern what was good from my past if I continued to lie in the present. I began to think of my mother. When the weekends came and went, and I was back home, she never commented on where I'd been. Not once. First I had been bothered by it, and then I understood it was, whether she intended or not, the beginning of our necessary separation. I made a left on Duane Street, where I stopped at a security booth that appeared to be empty. I twisted my neck to the left and the image of a black slab, so smooth it seemed wet, caused my legs to halt. It was one story tall with the white outline of a sankofa.

I could see the shape, though it was nighttime, because of how deeply the white paint was branded into the stone. It stood out against the tall metallic government buildings. As I walked toward the tablet, jumping the gate, I made out the words "For all those who were lost, For all those who were stolen, For all those who were left behind, For all those who were not forgotten." It seemed to be a monument to the transatlantic slave trade. A walkway appeared in front of me. It spiraled downward, so I followed it, touching each of the panels that appeared to my left, each one bearing a religious symbol. The panels stopped at a map of the earth with Mauritania at its center. Though the monument appeared to be a stone slab, from this angle it opened like the mouth of a fish. I ascended the short flight of stairs inside of it. There was another hole in the cave's ceiling about the size of the entrance. The sky was blank from that angle, each star removed by human pollution. I backed out of the enclosure to stare up, my ears pounded by what seemed to be the beating of sixty wings. As I exited the monument, the flaps turning to a hum, I saw the *nyame biribi wo soro*, which means that god is in the heavens. It was above the entrance.

As I looked up, beyond the symbol, there was no bird in sight. I went over to the grassy mounds on the right and sensed that I was sitting above the bones of former slaves. Fear overtook me. Everything seemed out of place and time. I had become upset while looking at that monument—*reach back and get it*. I backed out of the site, hopped the gate, and headed toward the A train, knowing exactly where to go next.

DECEMBER 13, 2009

The house had a new iron gate installed at the front door last April. It had arrived one month before I went to Melody's school to deliver the note. There were six bars—five were vertical, one was twisted and bisected the frame horizontally. There were five sankofa, three below the crossbar facing down, two above it facing upward. My mother came to the door in her pajamas and looked beyond me. I followed her into the kitchen, took a cigarette from her bowl, and lit it by the window in the living room. She stopped washing the teakettle.

"When did you start smoking?" No response. "You can't hear me talking to you?"

"No."

She smiled her condescending smile and continued to dry the kettle. "How was class?"

"All right."

"Nothing new and exciting?"

"No."

"Well, that's interesting."

"Where did you get the gate?"

Avoiding my eyes, she paused before putting the kettle on the plastic dish rack.

"Why?"

"I keep seeing sankofa in gates around New York City."

"San what?"

"You know what I'm talking about. The symbol in your gate. It's a sankofa."

She refilled the kettle with water before asking, "Are you going to keep smoking that cigarette?"

"Would you prefer me to put it out?"

The patients still arrived regularly in the summertime, though her winter appointments had begun to dwindle, and she was steadfast in her refusal to pay for more classes. That was the cause of my frustration, I thought, before seeing that this was one small reproach in a never-ending series I suffered at her hand. I put the cigarette out. "I keep seeing these West African symbols, and I can't figure out the connection between the white architects and the gates."

Doris put the pot on the stove again, turning on the gas burner before wiping some crumbs from the counter into her hand. "Wrought-iron gates became fashionable in Europe during the eighteenth century," she said. "Maybe the connection is between the Berbers and Masons, but I do not know."

"But the symbols are Akan. Why would Iberians or Continental Europeans have anything to do with it?"

"Maybe the sankofa is not just an Akan symbol. Maybe it developed in conjunction with other styles of the time—maybe some northern Islamic cultures." She chose every word carefully; her repetition of "maybe" was meant to irritate me. "Maybe 'West Africa,'" and she raised her fingers, "is not a remote cultural island," she said, acknowledging that she had known the sankofa. Her question, "San what," was meant only to bide time for a response. I picked up the cigarette and lit it again. She did not acknowledge the smoke but grabbed two mugs from the cabinet, staying there, at the farthest possible distance from me, before asking, "When did you become so angsty?"

"When did you start treating me like a patient, Doris?" She did not like that. "What's wrong, Doris?"

"Stop calling me by my first name." I put the cigarette out again, feeling more childish this time. She took the chamomile tea from the cabinet, then stared at me. I closed the distance between us to two feet.

"You are my mother."

"I know that."

"Why do I have to call you Aunt Doris?"

"That's just when my patients are here."

"Why?"

"Is that important?" She glided around me into the living room to turn the television on. "Do you call me aunt when it is only the two of us?"

"No."

"So, what is wrong with you?"

"This is not normal."

"A lot of shit isn't normal."

"You—"

"Do you pay the bills here? Did you pay for those writing classes? How do you think all of this is paid for? So you have to call me aunt sometimes, consider it the cost of living."

"I am your fucking son."

"You can't afford to talk the way you do." She picked up the remote and crept toward me. "Did you hear me?" Doris was in my face, pressing the plastic into the top row of teeth beneath my cheek. I stepped back, walked down the stairs to my bedroom, and bolted the door.

A car pulled into the driveway, interrupting my sleep.

DECEMBER 23, 2009

"I want to tell you the story of your birth again. Maybe I didn't say it enough. Maybe you didn't believe me. But I will say it again while we are both calm like this. I am Doris Tatum. I was born Doris Wesley. My parents are from Virginia. There is not much for me to tell you about that concerning yourself. I went to New York City as a twenty-something-year-old to get a degree in theology from City College. In my junior year, I met a man named Dennis Tatum on 130th Street and St. Nicholas Avenue. He was about twenty-five years older than me. He had attended a service by Dr. Calvin Butts on Sunday, and he had too much to say about it. In between words, I could see he suffered from a loneliness I found endearing. Dennis had moved out to Long Island from Harlem, in order to start his own ministry. He would let me stay some weekends at his house without bringing much controversy to his congregation. We married in 1983, and I lived with him for five years before he passed away from colon cancer. In our time together, he got me interested in the other side of the Abrahamic tradition—extending back to Egypt—which I had not known, since our people were Protestant and militaristic, like most working-class black families from Virginia. He left this house to me. In the beginning, some of his congregants would give me gifts. In the beginning, it was like he was here, and then it was not. I never much liked the beach, and I wanted to go back to the city and finish my degree.

"I got an apartment on 127th Street and St. Nicholas, which was like hell in 1989. Sometime in the winter, I began having these dreams about birth. It started with an image of Harriet Tubman coming from Dennis's ear. Next was Isis the redeemer, and then Erzuli the beautiful, then Sophia, with her legs open, birthing the demiurge. I stayed up late and rose late but snapped out of my spell just in time to sign up for classes. Somewhere near the end of March 1990 I found someone to sleep with me. He was a student from Brownsville, Brooklyn. I didn't love him past the small ways he reminded me of Dennis. That man was your father. His name was Jesse. That is your middle name, which I gave you so that you could never forget this story."

It was the explanation I'd heard throughout my youth, yet now there were questions I wanted to ask. "How did you choose him?"

"He liked me, and he was younger."

"Why younger?"

"So he could forget."

"Was he black?"

"That doesn't matter. Race is a construct. And you are my son, so you are black."

"But was he black?"

"He was mixed. Is that all? Does that meet your standards of truth?"

I shrugged.

"Now let me tell you something else. After you graduate from high school, I don't want you coming back here. You can come visit me but you will not live here during your school breaks, do you understand me?"

DECEMBER 24, 2009

I gazed east, down the platform at Bridgehampton, awaiting the oncoming headlights of the Long Island Rail Road train. The sun shone dimly through a layer of cirrus clouds.

Melody: Can you come over for Christmas? 12:48 p.m.
Me: I'm coming over tonight. 12:49 p.m.

In the train car, I sat next to a man who was wearing a blue pinstriped suit, his hair gelled back. He checked his phone from time to time, but rarely responded to messages. I got off at Penn Station and switched to the A train, traveling three stops to 125th Street, as I had done every Saturday morning since the beginning of September.

Melody: What time? 3:43 p.m.

I left the train and walked up St. Nicholas Terrace, to the eastern gate of City College, the university Doris purported to have attended. I tried to browse "City College architecture" on the phone, but the inquiry did not return any websites that seemed relevant. I entered the Wille Administration Building on Convent Avenue and looked up class records, 1978–1981 and 1989–1992. As I suspected, there was no Doris Wesley or Doris Tatum, so I left the building, walking downhill past the park and a cop car on 129th Street to 127th Street—the block I told Melody I was living on. Once there, I turned right, counting the building numbers, 356, 358, 360, as I had on the day I first visited, stopping to stare at the burned-down building, number 362. I smoked one of the four cigarettes I had stolen from Doris, as I always had. Then I went east to St. Nicholas Avenue and got on the A train at 125th Street.

Me: Now. 6:13 p.m.

Rick answered the door. "Are you still mad at me?" I wasn't sure what he was talking about at first, but I remembered that we had not seen each other since he gave me the key to the safe house.

"No."

"Good."

"Can I come in?"

"Of course." He moved out of the way. "I didn't mean to offend you. You know that, right?"

"Stop harassing him, Rick."

"We were just talking."

"You know he's my boyfriend." Her father looked away from me as if he just realized I hadn't come to see him.

"Of course he is."

She took my hand in hers and asked him, "Can I borrow forty dollars? We want to eat dinner."

"Of course." He reached into his pocket and gave her a hundred-dollar bill. We went to the Japanese restaurant across the street from her apartment, then to the Lincoln Square movie theater to see a romantic Bollywood film about a Mumbai teen on a game show who falls under investigation for knowing the answers. I wanted to talk to her about the things she had read in my notebook, which could lead me to telling her about my real life, but when I brought it up she pointed at the screen and said, "Art is art." As we crossed Broadway after the film, there were still no words. When was the right time to tell the truth? The moment was always passing, the now becoming then, and the words I wanted to say could not change what she would do after I said them. Melody would leave me. I would be alone again—on Long Island with Doris. I tried to separate my desire for her from my desire for the world I wanted to be a part of. We didn't have sex before going to sleep. In the middle of the night, I was staring at the side of Melody's face. The shadows obscured her cheekbones, and from the side she appeared to be a black woman. I was disturbed to think that what she looked like to me now, asleep in the shadows, was what she always was. In the morning, I would tell her the truth.

DECEMBER 25, 2009

When I rolled over, Melody was already in the bathroom. The daylight weakened my resolve. I forced out of my head the image of her screaming, her father calling the cops. She came to the bed and kissed me on the lips, then said we were supposed to meet Rick downstairs. I dressed quickly and we got into the elevator.

A silver hatchback was waiting right out front at Fifty-eighth Street. Rick's coat was made of a mahogany fur; Melody's was a snowboarder's jacket with lime-green trimmings. I wore a black peacoat. Snow flurries dampened my hair and neck. She hopped into the driver's seat. As the car rolled past the Trump development, which was not the International Tower (although it was also on the Upper West Side), I had a memory of Doris driving me to Sunday school. I did not think the memory was real. We were both riding to church, and I asked Doris, "Mommy, how come Jesus is white?" She said, "Because we live in America." I did not believe that we had ever lived in Harlem at all. Rick interrupted my thought. "I figured today we could do this kind thing for the Harlem housing authority and then we could figure the rest of it out."

"Figure what out?" I said. Rick threw up his hands. I looked at Melody to see her reaction, but she just sat forward, clutching the wheel. We rode uptown in silence, got off the highway, turning right on 145th Street to Seventh Avenue, turning back west, past St. Borromeo Church on 141st Street and Adam Clayton Powell Jr. Boulevard. Rick gathered some packages from the trunk and we walked to the entrance of the Drew Hamilton Houses. There were three young black men outside; they looked up at me. Once inside, I met an elderly man who was convinced I was his nephew Virgil. His daughter assured me he said that to everyone. I went to hold his three-fingered hand. It was callused, but his veins were soft like a rotten orange. He sat in a wheelchair, a rough, brown blanket covering his legs; no one had cut his hair in months. He held my hand for a few minutes as we watched them arrange under the tree the presents Rick had brought. He whispered, "I knew you'd be back, Virgil. I knew we would touch each other again," and I tried not to be taken by his madness. "You were always such a handsome boy," he said, his mouth bent into a small oval. He squeezed out his words. "Sweet and kind . . . black, bittery, and white cold." His daughter said they were song lyrics by Charles Mingus. They passed through him from beyond.

As we traveled farther downtown, 141st, 139th, 135th, and Adam Clayton Powell, stopping at different apartments, giving gifts to black and Latino families, I became nauseated. Rick kept repeating, "This is good, isn't it? David, can you grab the door? My hands are full." Although the people whose houses we entered stayed the same shade—somewhere between brown and beige—white families began appearing once we got below 135th Street. I looked to Melody, who seemed to be feeling better about herself with each passing home. We continued downtown, 133rd, 131st, crossing west to St. Nicholas Avenue. We neared the neighborhood from my past and present. Rick could see me becoming nervous. He said, "We've just got a couple more, and then we can stop by your mother's house."

"Excuse me?"

"She is home on Christmas, is she not?"

As the car continued to move, my body felt removed—my life seemed removed from their lives.

"No," I said.

"Oh, quiet, it will be short," Rick said.

Though he had not asked to be welcomed into my home, he assumed his right to go there. I was upset by his words, but more so by my lie, which had caused this sequence of passive-aggressive actions that they hoped would lead to my mother. I knew there would be no resolution. The building I pretended to live in had not been reconstructed yet. I had to stop the trip before Melody found out I was a fraud. We got out on 130th Street and Adam Clayton Powell, three blocks from the apartment building where I had said I lived. Melody hustled in front of her father, opening the door for us. I ascended the stairs with a black garbage bag in my left hand that was filled with toys. He knocked on apartment 3c, declaring again, "This is good, isn't it?" Heat rose to my nostrils. Rick turned to look at me and, briefly, terror disrupted his face. I tried to calm down by staring at different objects in the hallway. There were radiators with chipped copper paint. There were yuletides and quotes of beatitude, little Jesuses with glowing red hearts, blessed Marys in pure white cloth. Melody's words about Rick, Rick's words about his father and the city's class structure, stared at me through the center of the yuletide on the door in front of us. I inhaled from the base of my nostrils. The mucus left my mouth and landed on the right side of her father's lip. I ran down the two flights of stairs, Melody's footsteps sounding behind me. A solitary wind gust swept up the avenue.

I looked back to 131st Street. "What's wrong with you?" Melody mouthed. I continued toward the station, but she did as well, so I had to sprint to 145th Street. I took the A twelve stops to Hoyt-Schermerhorn, transferring to the C train going east two stops to Clinton-Washington. I got out on the wrong side of the street, passed the restaurant that resembled a drugstore, and crossed at St. James Place. The block was quiet. I tapped once on the brick and took the key out.

Act
IV

I was thinking about retracing my footsteps from that day in November, when I had last seen the man in the gray suit. I reached the bench in front of the sign that read "Salmon Hole" again, and began to walk uphill. The wind blew in the other direction, as particles of frozen water got underneath my hood, turning to liquid droplets from the warmth, dripping down. They froze on my face. I passed the graveyard, the Medical Building, and the undergraduate dorms on Trinity Campus, keeping my eyes on the sky. Airplanes sounded above, though I could not see them; buses and cars hummed by. The cold isolated each tone so that the sounds of the world were bound and unobtrusive. To my right there was a purple house with pink polka dots, which had CUT CONSUMPTION NOT FORESKINS written across it in large white letters. As I reached the corner of Prospect Street, where North turns to South, I walked toward the entrance of Ira Allen Chapel, again. I stood in front of two large wooden doors, glancing up at the lamp by the entrance. The doors were locked. I looked down at the phone.

Ira Allen was the founder of the University of Vermont, though he had been removed from the founding narrative for close to a century. He had been unable to pay the money he'd pledged to the Vermont legislature for the school he had helped to charter, so he traveled to France (1795) to raise funds. His strategy was to arm Vermonters and Canadians with ten thousand guns from the French Directory and secede from the United States. He would then create "United Columbia," and use his position in the new government to pay down his debts. The French agreed. Allen boarded a ship with the arms, but as his boat left French waters for America, it was stopped and detained by Great Britain. By direction of the newly formed United States government, the British imprisoned Ira for three years. When he was deported back to Vermont, he was arrested again and put in debtor's prison. Once back in his home state Ira escaped from jail, disgraced and homeless.

In 1809, he appeared in the diary of a North Texas man fighting for Mexican independence. Though Ira was an ineffective soldier—his joints would seize in pain, sending him into spastic fits—he could not return home because he remained a fugitive in Vermont. On January 15, 1814, the university's founder passed away in Philadelphia and was interred in a pauper's grave. Had it not been for the oration of the Latin professor John Goodrich (1892), Ira Allen might never have been memorialized at the university. Though the story had interested me, it did not connect to the man in the gray suit, so I closed the Internet browser and continued past Old Mill and the Royall Tyler Theatre—where I could just make out the light blue water tower that hovered above campus to the east.

Me: I still want to speak to you. David. 8:15 p.m.

I slid the key into the dorm room door, and no one greeted me. I put my backpack down, went over to the tan dresser, and looked out the window. From that vantage point, I counted heads almost all evening—every student I saw leave returned about every hour and a half. I thought about going down to the Rib Shack, but my time with Mark felt over for now. I wanted to lie down and stay that way until the morning washed over me again.

DECEMBER 8, 2010

When I woke, the orange container stood on my desk, menacing. I had taken a pill the morning before, and was suffering that same indecision I felt then, before swallowing another. I walked into the atrium of my dorm and went to the front desk to get my mail. I picked through the letters from the school disciplinary committee, the statements from Wells Fargo, and the other two, from a branch of the U.S. Department of Education, but did not find anything from Doris. I put the letters in my backpack and walked to see Amelia at the Student Health Center's offices.

"How's your mother?"

"Fine."

"Is she still struggling with addiction?"

"No, that was just the lie I'd told Melody."

"Have you told her the truth?"

"The truth?"

"That you are not who you said you were?" It was becoming apparent that this session would lead to others, and I would develop the belief that my mental health was dependent on her counsel.

"I did it over break," I lied.

"How did Melody react?"

"She wasn't happy."

"But how did she react?"

"She didn't believe that Doris was my mother."

"Where were you? How did you say it? Give me the details."

"We were in the safe house; I remember that."

"If this happened over Thanksgiving break you shouldn't have trouble remembering the events." I was beginning to believe this school was holding a little file on me that would become a public record. I didn't want to talk about it. We moved on. "Have you written anything since the last time we spoke?"

"No."

"Why not?"

"It's too painful to make sense of."

"What is it?"

"Life."

"Maybe you should try to write in the present tense."

"I've tried to switch tense before—"

"No, like, write about now."

"No."

"Why not?"

"The monotony of life doesn't allow me to think critically about the present."

"Have you tried the ALANA house?"

"No."

"You should go to their Friday brunch. It might be good for you. How have the antidepressants been working?"

"I don't notice a difference yet."

"Let me know on the next visit if there are still no changes." I agreed and then walked back to the dorm.

Snowflakes fell behind the glass entrance. I began to remember again how I had left Melody on that day in Harlem, in the cold, so I tried to send her a message, but the phone service had been cut off. I sat down at a booth in the atrium of my dorm, which was connected to a hallway that led from Amelia's office. In the seat next to me, there was a newspaper dated November 30, 2010. I began reading about the implementation of the Transdisciplinary Research Initiative (TRI), which was not popular among professors who did not work in fields that could be described as complex systems, food systems, neuroscience, or behavior and health. I brought the paper back upstairs, unlocked the door, and placed it on the bed before riffling through the different issues of *The Cynic*, volume 127, that I had collected in my room. September 14, 2010, was underneath Gary's old bed, so I skimmed through it, remembering most articles, like "Future of Centennial Questioned." I looked at volume 127, issue 5, noticing a piece about the president's search for a new provost that dominated the front page. At the bottom left corner of page 4 there was an advertisement for People's United Bank. To the right of this ad was the article entitled "Professors Comment on the History of Kake Walks." It continued: "Kake Walks and Dance Competitions: Race and Performance in American Popular Culture ... the final event marking the launch of the Center for Digital Initiatives' new digital collection 'Kake Walk at UVM' took place Oct. 4 in Royall Tyler Theatre." I read on: "This addresses the race issue and allows for a serious study of race that can help us to understand 'whiteness,' Gennari said." I put down the paper, pacing, then put my jacket on and walked to the library.

I pointed the mouse at >>CLICK HERE FOR KAKE WALK<<, which directed me to the college's sponsored page. I began searching through the images tab of the Digital Collection to see if I could find Rick's father, but I did not. The pictures were making me upset, so I thought to look through the *Cynic* archive, beginning with the year on the picture Melody had shown me, 1954. It was the same year that the Supreme Court ruled in favor of Brown v. the Board of Education of Topeka. The ruling rejected segregation. I typed "Kake Walk University of Vermont 1954" into the library's computer. I clicked on the annual magazine (February 1954) the school sent around as a recap of the weekend's events. The cover page featured two white men in pink suits, with their hands in the air and black paint strategically masking their faces—except around their eyes and mouths, which were painted white for contrast. I clicked to the second page and in the left column an ad read, "Look at the Front Page again, look at the black face, this is the tradition that we want to see ended!" Right next to this ad was an article that stated, "Two Months of Speculation Went into Selecting News-paper's Front Page." I looked inside that section for some contin-uation, perhaps, some initiation of the debate about blackface; instead, the article focused on the difficulties of printing in color. I searched the pages for more dissent, finding "Psychology Prof. Finds Numerous Motives Behind Kakewalk Affair . . . Some con-sider what goes on at Kake Walk a sign of immaturity, emotion-ality, and irresponsibility, while others—more tolerant—view it as merely an aspect of the general social life at college with a let-them-have-fun-while-they-may attitude." I realized the second-page ad was what the archive had meant by "the begin-ning of student dissent." It was evident the alumni and adminis-tration either had no idea a Kake Walk was the end of the minstrel show's second act, or they had no desire to recognize their tradition as such. There was a letter to the editor post-marked "Dixie" from a small town in Florida. "The U.S. census shows Vermont has 519 negroes. 519! We have 880,000 of these Africans in our state. If it were not for Ed Sullivan, those Ver-mont syrup people would never have seen a Negro." I went through all the magazines, reading for signs of dissent until "The 1964 Kake Walk Ushers in a New Look for Walkers," sure there would be change in the year that the Civil Rights Act had been passed. When I saw the pictures in black-and-white print, the men still appeared to be in blackface. On page 5, the university president addressed the student body: "After extended delibera-tion, the interfraternity council and its constituent fraternities have decided that blackface shall be replaced by green face, and the kinky hair wigs shall be retired, although it was never meant to be offensive."

"Excuse me, sir?" I turned in my seat. "The library is closed."

I looked at the man in front of me, who had suffered a disfigurement of the spine. I apologized and left briskly, though I had not found what I was searching for.

<h2 style="text-align:center">DECEMBER 9, 2010</h2>

"How have you been?" Dr. Hume inquired.

"I haven't refilled the prescription."

"Why not?"

"I'm embarrassed to go to the pharmacy."

He touched the place where his heart would be on his lab coat. I thought for sure he was mocking me until he rested that hand on my shoulder.

"No one is saying this is forever. Just for now."

"Maybe they aren't for me."

He rifled through his pocket, searching for a pen. "Are you having suicidal thoughts?"

"No."

"Have you increased or decreased your drug intake?"

"Excuse me?"

"Illicit drugs?"

"About the same. Less, possibly."

"It's not an ideal solution for everyone, but they have been proven to work. Let us just restart on the twenty and up it to thirty in a month. It seems like the trial worked. No changes in mood, correct?"

"I don't dream anymore."

"Everyone dreams."

"I don't remember my dreams."

"That's fine. I'm sure your dreams will return." He paused. "But tell me if they don't." I plodded upstairs, stopping next to an ax encased in glass before exiting the building. I did not want to refill my prescription. Outside, the temperature was well below freezing. There were not many students around. In between South Prospect and University Place, I walked by a blond girl with sharp features who was laughing with a friend. She glanced at me, then continued to giggle. It made me think of the connection between eugenics, the College of Medicine, and me. I could not help but feel I was being aided down some long and winding path that would result in my ritual sterilization.

I typed "1969" into the browser on the library's computer, knowing it was the last year the school sponsored the Kake Walk. I began scanning through each article in the February magazine that was solely devoted to the Kake Walk. There was no outright denunciation. There was no inflamed critic taking a scythe to the documents, exposing wrongdoing by members of the administration or student body, just muted pieces such as "Pops Night—a Success?" or "Arena Theater to Present *Antigone*." The journalists barely mention this momentous change in the school's history. I went back and forth, rereading Xerox's ad, "Equal opportunity employer (m/f)," and others like it. Near page 17, there was an article that revealed the results of a poll detailing whether the student body wanted to end the Kake Walk weekend. Sixty-six percent said they did not. Toward the end of the paper, I read, "Black Literature Course to Be Offered . . . The English Department has announced it will offer a course in American Negro Literature in the Fall," and was reminded of Jean Toomer's *Cane*. I sat at the window, envisioning the time before 1969 when there were fewer than a thousand copies of the novel in circulation. Jean Toomer had not published a word since 1950. He died in obscurity in 1967, three months before *Loving v. Virginia* legalized interracial marriage—two years before Harper's would republish his work. The company had capitalized on two things: the need for the university system to validate "legitimate" black expression, and a growing college marketplace (student population ca. 1923—947,000; ca. 1970—8,500,000) to consume it. How do you legitimize a human construct? First, it had to be separated. But what is the impact of separating American Negro literature from American literature? The history of Toomer spoke against this binary, but that was not significant. His work endured as a symbol, representing a movement he did not want to be identified with.

I found *Cane* on the second floor and took it from the shelf. The cover bore the profile of a boy's face without an ear. Inside this outline, there were three black planters in the southern sun, each wearing a straw hat. This was Harper's 1969 iteration. I sat back down at the public computers, leafing through the chapters, stopping nowhere in particular. I turned to the story "Theater" to read about Dorris, as I had usually done, and the previous owner or loaner of the book had written "Write!" in the margin. I focused on this note, then closed the book. Though I expected these thoughts to lead me to an epiphany, I was soon disappointed. Still no man in the gray suit. I left the library, finding there were other students outside. It was cold, so most people had pulled their hoods tight around their faces. Looking at my peers, I could not discern individual features, just white faces that were a combination of faces I had seen before. As I continued passing by the campus buildings, with their European façades, I noticed that every single person grinned at me. Smiled, mocking, as if I were on the receiving end of some long and deliberate joke. I tried to distinguish each individual as they passed but was overwhelmed by the similarities. The school and students were defined by one contiguous style, I thought. Whiteness. The architect: colonial amnesia.

My dorm window looked out upon a freshman green. There were pizza boxes and dirty socks around the room. I remembered the mess that was my life. Outside, a young man wearing a tan duffle coat strolled with a young woman in a brown jacket. He was laughing, tilting his head so that the light caught the golden strands in his hair. She leaned into him; they pecked, then separated. Three branches and a green frame, which cut the window into ten panels, impeded the view. At that moment a bluebird, from seasons past, arrived from thin air and perched on the third, the least strong, branch I peeked over the covers at my notebook in the wastebasket. As I craned my neck to look out the window again, the sun had already fallen well below the horizon. I walked across campus to Jeffords Hall, where I could follow the path indoors through Stafford Hall and the health-and-science research facility. I walked through rooms, finding silent technicians in different stages of experimentation. They looked surprised when I appeared but, recognizing me as a fellow student, immediately went back to work as if I had not interrupted. The lack of security seemed odd, but for whom, against whom, I thought, continuing into the atrium of the Given Medical Building. I stopped and turned to my left. There was a wall of medical school graduation pictures. Every student had been photographed since the beginning of the twentieth century. The black frames stretched up two stories and the pictures at the top faded from view. I walked backward until I could see each face. From the left side of the wall, the images were marked by the year of graduation and the name. I followed the years as they rose—'12, '13 . . . '18 . . . '22, until I got to '55. Once there, I scanned each of the photos: '55 Dylan West, '55 Perry Stephens, '55 Kyle Munch, '55 Richard Murzynowics. I was entranced. His hair was parted on the left, and it waved over to the right. His eyes were close to the bridge of his nose. I looked at the photo for a while, calling to mind the other image of him that I had seen. I searched Richard's expression for anger, for something beneath the surface, but staring back at me was a college student from the 1950s who didn't much resemble Melody's father. I imagined him walking to Simpson Hall, waiting at the front desk for his Kake Walk date. I saw him sleeping in the bedroom of 282 South Prospect Street, where I had the first vision of the man in the gray suit. I envisioned Richard passing Ira Allen Chapel, then Billings Library, into the center of campus, looking up to Converse Hall, feeling he had achieved some great act of survival, not realizing it would eat at him, in small bites, for the rest of his days. In a way, I had come to the school to discover this same truth, though it was something I had already known. I looked down and suffered feelings of loneliness. I saw an image of myself. It was hitting its head against a wall, in the same manner, over and over again. My emotions left me wanting company, so I descended the hill toward the lake, turned north on Willard Street, and walked into the Rib Shack, where there were two handles of whiskey on the table.

When Mark saw me, he said, "Look!"

James, Matthew, and Luke turned, already drunk, repeating, "The prodigal son has returned," in different, whining pitches. We laughed together. One of the bottles was almost finished, the other was half finished, and only the four of them were in the house. I sat down, and we all began repeating, "Pass the whiskey, pass the whiskey." Matt got up to vomit in the bathroom. The game was to not let the whiskey touch the table. "Pass the whiskey, pass the whiskey." Luke created an early 2000s hip-hop playlist, and the living room was filled with the voices of black men, again. For twenty minutes (the second bottle was finished) we all rapped the words—them omitting *nigger* because I was there. But every *nigger* they omitted built the tension in the living room (the first bottle was finished), until I heard Matt screaming, "Nigger! Nigger!" in the kitchen.

I rounded the corner as Mark said, "What are you doing?"

Matt turned to me and said, "I'm not calling him a nigger. I'm not even using the word *nigger*."

"So what are you doing?" I asked.

"I am saying *niggar* with an *a*. You know. Like something that is worthless." But Matt had not inflected the *e* any differently than the *a*. He smiled at me and put his head through the Sheetrock next to their bathroom. His nose was cut and bleeding. Mark was speechless. I realized that what Matt had meant to say was *niggardly*, though the word meant cheap, not worthless.

"Where are you going, bro?"

If I could have laughed along with them—felt detached enough from the historical concept of a nigger, or the disgust I felt when it came from a white man's mouth—I would have. We had been approaching this crossroads since we engaged in a friendship, and the end was not as hurtful as it was embarrassing. I had not seen it coming. I relegated us to minor actors in a greater tribal play, and continued along, crossing Pearl Street to University Place, where the cold began to creep beneath my jacket. I crossed the campus green until the road reached a fork. There was a statue of our school's founder, Ira Allen, at the crossroads. It was not the first memorial to stand on that patch of the green. Before Allen, there had been the Marquis de Lafayette, whose name is used on many streets in the United States of America, notably in lower Manhattan. I had traversed it last December. The statue was erected in 1883 alongside renovations to the Old Mill (High Victorian Gothic) that remade the face of the old Old Mill (Federal). Four years after the school erected the statue that still stood at this crossroads, McKim, Meade & White had finished constructing the Ira Allen Chapel (Colonial Revival), the building I had been called to in November. As I stared up, the figure reminded me of Teddy Roosevelt's monument outside the Museum of Natural History, though the two men were memorialized in different positions, at different years of age. The statue was erected in 1925, during Prohibition, and in February of 1958, it was defaced.

It was as if a mist covered the present. All that came before informs us, and is then obscured by us. I stepped off the base of the statue and walked backward. Above Allen's head, I could see the frames of all the buildings on campus: Federal, Greek Revival, Italianate Revival, High Victorian Gothic, Richardsonian Romanesque, Queen Anne Revival, Victorian Eclectic, Neoclassical Revival, Colonial Revival, Art Deco, International, Brutalist, Postmodern. They appeared as one building in my mind, and as I was drawn back to the figure of Ira Allen, a mist was coming from his chest. A man pushed out of his sternum and walked toward the Living and Learning Complex, which linked Central to the athletic campus. I followed, turning right with him, past the murals in remembrance of the U.S. military's presence in El Salvador, September 11, and Earth Day. He

walked south, crossing the amphitheater, then the outdoor basketball courts, to the gym, where lights were still on though it
was the dead of night. I continued to follow as he broke into a
sprint. I was running, too. Our footsteps echoed against the
buildings. The clack of his dress shoes seemed to repeat the
thud of my sneakers. He stopped behind a blue Chevrolet Im-
pala, pulled something out of his pocket, and went around the
other side of the car. I could see letters appearing on the wind-
shield but could not make out the words. When I shuffled
around the automobile, the man in the gray suit was no longer
there. I bent down and read his handwriting—"We wear the
mask that —— and lies." The red words and dash were sus-
pended in the dark. I remembered the verse from Paul Lau-
rence Dunbar's "We Wear the Mask" (1896). Dunbar's name was
used to replace the "M" school in Washington, D.C., in 1916. It
was where, seven years prior, Jean Toomer had become con-
scious of his blackness. I began to recite the poem.

> "We wear the mask that grins and lies,
> It hides our cheeks and shades our eyes, —
> This debt we pay to human guile;
> With torn and bleeding hearts we smile . . ."

I thought: "To grin is a red herring that distracts you from a lie.
To lie is a red herring that distracts you from the truth." Before
I could dissect the meaning of the omission of "grins," I had
stopped moving again. There was no unified thing he was
showing me, no reason I should be obsessing over his actions,
so I looked around the parking lot, dark and empty, then continued behind Patrick Gymnasium and Gutterson Arena, toward my dorm room. I opened 321, and papers wrapped around

my ankles. I laid my head to rest, waking to the toothbrush on my desk, which I'd used twenty times all semester. I decided to clean my teeth.

There was a copy of the school's newspaper on the bathroom sink. The new provost had denied the student body the right to see course evaluations. I remembered the very first issue of this volume, number 127, where the president of the student government sat smiling, defying the institution's right to hide reviews of teachers, then the third issue, where the congress slandered his name for this executive action. On page 6 there was an article about the Royall Tyler Theatre hosting *Harry Potter*, the play. The three witches of Macbeth appeared in my head. They were singing around a cauldron with black-faced dancers, peering into their future and our past. My mental associations no longer weighed me down, so I continued reading without stopping to feel. The pills were beginning to suppress the guilt I needed to interpret my emotions. On page 8 there was a piece about an amusing end-of-semester ritual that students had invented in the '90s, next to a small opinion piece entitled "Call a Plumber, My Wiki Is Leaking." The two articles were separated by one black line. I read both stories, without regard for their boundaries.

"Whether you bike, run, | The oil leak in the Gulf | long board, rollerblade, skip, dance or | Coast of the United States may | hop, the Naked Bike Ride allows you | not in fact be the largest and | to express yourself in one of the most | most destructive leak that we | liberating ways possible. | have seen this year." The point was not to try to perceive reality as it was presented, but all at once, without the burden of history. I went back to the dorm room and found a box of garbage bags on my former roommate's desk. I put the last three pills in one of them, before adding the phone that Rick had given me. I saw the wastebasket in the corner and pulled my notebook from it. The pieces of my novel were too short and too disconnected to be considered chapters. Some of the sentences were crossed out and written over. The six entries and the Prologue were all right, but the work needed something else, a narrator outside of me, maybe, a theme to fill out the sketches. I picked up the blue pen on my desk, then put both pen and notebook in the garbage bag, before leaving all of the trash beside the welcome mat. At the base of the stairway, I saw groups of students huddled around tables in the atrium. Some of them were studying. I walked in their direction, headed toward the entrance.

The sunlight shone from outside, so I closed my eyes and imagined Melody there. She was waiting now. A distance separated us, though we were not far apart. I tried to hold on to the image but the vision was passing. I raised my eyelids.

Acknowledgments

I would like to thank my parents, Wynton, Candace, and Greg. I would like to thank my siblings, Wynton, Jasper, Sydney, Cameron, and Oni. I would like to thank all the Tatums, Stanleys, Marsalises, and Ferdinands, wherever you are. Without you this work would not have been possible. I would like to thank my closest friends, and, Shhh . . .

I would also like to acknowledge everyone at Catapult for making this book a tangible object and supporting it. A special thanks to Zachary Lazar, who helped turn my early effort into a contiguous novel. Finally, I would like to thank my editor, Pat Strachan, for turning that contiguous novel into *As Lie Is to Grin*.